Growl at the Moon
A Weird Western

Growl at the Moon
A Weird Western

Rhys Hughes

First published in 2024 by
Telos Publishing, 139 Whitstable Road, Canterbury,
Kent CT2 8EQ, United Kingdom.
www.telos.co.uk

ISBN: 978-1-84583-238-4

Telos Publishing Ltd values feedback. Please e-mail
any comments you might have about this book to:
feedback@telos.co.uk

Growl at the Moon
© Rhys Hughes, 2024

Cover © 2024 David J Howe

The moral right of the author has been asserted.

British Library Cataloguing in Publication Data.
A catalogue record for this book is available from the
British Library.

This book is sold subject to the condition that it shall
not by way of trade or otherwise, be lent, resold,
hired out or otherwise circulated without the
publisher's prior written consent in any form of
binding or cover other than that in which it is
published and without a similar condition including
this condition being imposed on the subsequent
purchaser.

Contents

Chapter One: Mad Mister Meteor   7
Chapter Two: Jalamity Kane   41
Chapter Three: Chain Of Command   88
Chapter Four: Dog Face Chief   137
Chapter Five: The Cliché Hunter   151
Chapter Six: Monkey Man Manor   166
Chapter Seven: Sideliners   219
Chapter Eight: Gunsmith Ghouls   241

This novel is dedicated to my wife, Maithreyi.

Chapter One
Mad Mister Meteor

The crescent moon was so thin that it looked like a sickle blade up there in a sky almost empty of clouds. But the only mind hoping to reap a harvest at this time of night belonged to the dark figure on the roof of the bank. He used a crowbar to force open a skylight and so skilled was he at this kind of work that no sound disturbed the peace of the town below.

He uncoiled a rope and secured one end to the crenelated parapet. Then he dropped the line into the space he had exposed. Down the rope he went with the agility of a spider on a silken thread, his bag of tools slung over one shoulder. It was a silent operation. Time passed, maybe half an hour. Then a side door at the base of the building silently opened and the figure emerged. He had managed to pick half a dozen locks from the inside.

He was carrying a sack in his arms now, as well as his own bag, and that is why he was a little less sure on his feet. He lurched around a corner, hurrying to the place he had hitched his horse, and he lumbered straight into an obstacle that made him drop both his burdens. He blinked. It was dark in this street and what stood before him was hidden in shadow.

But his eyes adjusted quickly and he soon saw that he was facing a man in the murk. He wanted to cry out but he controlled himself. After all, what should he have to fear if he played it cool? 'If you'll permit me to pass,' he said, 'then I would be most obliged. Thank you.'

And he smiled and supposed that his teeth gleamed sufficiently in not an unfriendly fashion. But the obstacle said nothing in reply, merely watched him with inscrutable eyes. There was no true animosity in that gaze but no warmth either. The thief suddenly felt very cold.

The stranger was stooped and wore a cowl over his head, but the force of the collision had shifted the cowl a little and a few wisps of white hair could be glimpsed. An old man? Somehow the thief doubted it. There was a strangeness about him that no oldtimer possessed.

Beyond the stranger, the thief's horse pawed the ground and he guessed he could make a dash for it. He picked up his bag of tools, revealing no anxiety in his voice as he did so, though his hands shook. 'No harm done,' he said with as pleasant a lilt as he could manage.

Then he struck, rapidly too. He swung the heavy bag at the man who stood before him and let go of the handle at the same time. His opponent uttered not a word but fell back a few steps under the impact, and then the thief grabbed his other piece of luggage, the sack, and ran for his horse. He was in the saddle in a flash, the sack resting against the pommel before him, his heels jerking into the stallion's flanks. His laughter rang out.

His steed was agile and strong, a suitable mount for an individual as fast, athletic and daring as he. He counted himself safe now he was galloping out of town and heading for the wilds. He was confident he could elude any search party that might be sent after him. He was sure he could make good his escape from any posse this town could muster.

After all, he was Danny Bangs, the slickest, quickest burglar of the age, a criminal who had never been caught. His early training had been in an itinerant circus as an acrobat, then he joined a gang of outlaws in the far north, learning stamina as well as flexibility, and now he worked for the man he knew only as The Lord, who kept him on his toes by giving him very difficult tasks indeed, and by so doing ensured that he remained at the very peak of his powers. Nobody could catch Danny when he was riding.

Thus it was with some consternation that he heard the hooves behind him and realised they were gaining, not dropping behind. He urged his horse to yet greater effort, and he wondered who his pursuer might be. The only plausible possibility was that it was the stranger he had attacked with his tool bag. What had the fellow been doing anyway, standing so still in that narrow street? Was he one of the sheriff's deputies? Perhaps he was also a thief planning to break into the bank! Coincidences do happen.

No, he couldn't be a deputy, his shape was all

wrong, stooped over like a worn-out prospector who'd never had any luck in his life. And the white gloves he wore on his hands! That surely wasn't normal, not around these parts, and Danny didn't like to think about it. But none of this was important. Escaping with the loot was all that truly mattered.

Danny pulled on his reins and turned his horse towards the maze of rocks known as *Los Gigantes Rotos*, the Broken Giants, that travellers preferred to avoid. The hundreds of huge boulders were perfect for throwing his pursuer off the scent, especially with so little moonlight. There were many apparent routes through the maze but most of them ended in dead ends. Danny had familiarised himself with them all as a precaution.

It was therefore with astonishment bordering on terror that he turned one towering mass of rock twenty minutes later and found himself hurtling into the same obstruction as before, the cowled stranger immobile on his own horse, a gun suddenly appearing in his gloved hand, his eyes still staring without malice, mercy or curiosity. And Danny screamed.

Punta Arena is a tiny settlement on the coast of California, and just south of it, balanced on the cliffs that fringe the shore, at latitude 38.8977°N precisely, was something known as The Lord, but it wasn't a man. It was a vast steel tube on a colossal frame and one end of the tube jutted out over the cliffs and the sea. It pointed at the sky at an angle that had been carefully calculated. It gleamed and sparkled menacingly in the sunlight.

The citizens of Punta Arena who bothered to walk down to take a look at it were told it was a telescope. But the labourers who had constructed it had been told something else entirely, and they had been told in strict secrecy, and most of them kept their mouths shut or echoed the official line that it was a telescope for observing the planets in great detail.

But there are always a few loose tongues in any gang and somehow it was leaked that the steel tube was a piece of artillery, a supergun, and that it had an urgent purpose, namely to protect the United States of America from an enemy on the far side of the ocean. The secret was openly admitted one afternoon when a visitor from Punta Arena happened to be passing. Jeb Smith stared at the tube, rubbed his eyes and shook his head.

The Lord was indeed a supergun and it had been designed and paid for by the man also known as The Lord, who issued his orders only by telegraph and was served loyally by two officers on site, Randall and Hardy. Nobody seemed able to say where this benefactor was located but it wasn't anywhere in California, and there was speculation he was based out East, maybe even in New York or Boston or another of those far off places.

Randall saw Jeb staring mesmerised at the device and he came out of the shack that served as his quarters. 'You're looking mighty confused,' he said in a friendly voice, a cigar clamped between his teeth. He blinked at Jeb and with a gesture at the tube, the visitor grinned.

'Spying on other planets, don't see the use of that.'

And he spat tobacco juice.

Randall saw no pressing need to keep the pretence up. He uttered a laugh and told Jeb, 'I'm sure there's a good reason why astronomers like to find out about the worlds of the universe, but this isn't an observatory. No, it's a cannon, a supergun, and it's pointed at our enemies.'

Jeb gazed out to sea and whistled. 'The sea is our enemy now? Times sure are changing.' He stuffed another wad of tobacco into his mouth. 'Some whales been threatening California maybe?'

'You are a comedian,' said Randall approvingly, 'and ought to be on stage in San Francisco. They'd like you down there. But let's be straight about this. I guess you heard of the Empire of Japan? They think the Pacific Ocean belongs to them. You know the latitude of this gun? No, I don't suppose you do exactly. It happens to be on the same latitude as the port city of Kesennuma in Japan. A large fleet is being assembled there.'

'You are telling me that this gun here is powerful enough to lob a shell all the way over the Pacific?' gasped Jeb.

Randall nodded and relit his cigar. He blew a smoke ring and watched it drift away inland on the gentle sea breeze.

'The most powerful gun ever,' he said proudly.

'A government project, is it?'

'Sure, but a secret one.'

'Well, the cat's out of the bag now.' And Jeb scratched his head and gazed up at the barrel again. 'A big cat.'

'The biggest,' said Randall, 'and I hope I have satisfied your curiosity. It's a case of national security, that's all.'

Jeb nodded, and having no more reason to linger there, he turned to begin the walk back to Punta Arena. Randall watched him depart and when he was an insignificant speck on the clifftop path, he returned to the shack, where Hardy was waiting with arched eyebrows. 'Well?'

'I told him it was government property. That ought to keep him quiet for a time. I don't think he's a threat to us.'

'None of those small-town fellas are,' agreed Hardy, 'and the news about a fleet in Japan really troubles them. My only concern is if a government agent turns up out of the blue, as they sometimes do, then the whole project is at risk and we'll be in very deep trouble.'

'Our task will be accomplished long before any inspector comes round to poke his nose into it,' Randall said.

Hardy nodded and they laughed together.

While they were laughing, a message came through on the telegraph line. A stock ticker on a desk in the corner started chattering and ticker tape spilled out of the device. Randall moved swiftly to snatch it up and read it as it was being printed. He glanced at Hardy.

'The Lord has more instructions for us.'
'It's time?' asked Hardy.
'Just awaiting delivery of the propellant.'
'How much longer?'
'The Lord says it's on its way.'

They both raised their heads to look through the only window in the shack, a circular pane of glass like a porthole that afforded them a view of the ocean and they imagined the huge artillery shell speeding through the atmosphere in a blaze of red-hot fury, vanishing over the line of the horizon on its way to smash a gargantuan crater in the port city where the enemy fleet was being prepared. It made them feel a mixture of emotions.

Danny crouched against the base of an especially twisted boulder and shook all over with fear. But so far the cowled man hadn't offered him violence. The gun was still in his gloved hand and it was pointing at Danny. Beneath the sickle of the moon, a reaping of the truth was taking place, but it was bloodless and the thief prayed it would remain that way.

The stranger had ordered the thief to dismount and he had opened the sack and peered inside, shaking his head and giving Danny a sardonic smile. 'Plenty of used banknotes in there,' he said, 'and something tells me they don't rightly belong to you. Safe cracker, are you?'

Danny nodded dumbly. For the first time in his career he felt defeated and it was an unpleasant sensation. How could such a fit and agile athlete end up at the mercy of a stooped figure with white hair? There was a mystery here that he didn't care to ponder too deeply. He was worried there might be a supernatural explanation for the stranger's existence.

'But you aren't an ordinary kind of burglar, are you? I heard tell of Danny Bangs and I was always intrigued by your abilities. I doubt you were stealing a sum as large as this just to keep yourself in whisky. Supposing I hogtie you and take you back to town and deliver you to the sheriff? Would you appreciate that and be grateful to me? I kinda doubt it.'

Danny said, with a trembling voice, 'Just money for myself. Planning to retire, get it? Want to set up a home, raise a family, live an upright life, even go to church regular and pay my taxes.'

'Now *that's* a farfetch'd tale, my friend. Why not just be honest. I have a special power, see. I know when I'm being told a lie and I don't like it much. It makes my finger itchy on a trigger.'

'Your finger?' For some reason Danny felt there was something unnatural about that gloved white hand, but he couldn't say what it was. Yet he believed a man as peculiar as this cowled stranger might have the power to know a lie from the truth. He sighed and shrugged.

'Have it your own way. I was hired.'

'Burglar for hire, huh? Who hired you, Danny? Not that it's strictly any of my business. But I didn't like the way you swung that bag of tools into my face and now I reckon you owe me one.'

'Maybe I do,' ruefully admitted Danny.

The Growl, for such was the name he was known by, said, 'If you hadn't struck at me, I would have let you pass.' He mused for a moment. 'That's one of the ironies of life. People make problems for themselves and then they make those problems worse. But just tell me who hired you and I don't think there'll be many unpleasant consequences.'

'The Lord, that's who,' blurted out Danny.

'Interesting nickname.'

'I don't know anything about him,' continued Danny without any further prompting, 'and I never even saw him. He gave me his orders via his officers and I was promised a percentage of the haul. That's all. The money in this sack is to pay a fella named Strongbow.'

'And why does he deserve to be paid?'

'I don't know, honestly I don't. Something to do with his work. He worked for The Lord, same as me, but he was a designer or a mathematician, not certain what, it's none of my business, see.'

'You only overheard snatches of conversation?'

'That's it exactly! Just so.'

The Growl stepped back and nodded at the

huddling Danny. 'Reckon you are telling the truth. Also reckon I'll take that sack off your hands and give the money to Strongbow myself. Problem is, I don't know what your destination is, except that it's west nor'west?'

'Punta Arena, California coast,' babbled Danny.

'In the town itself?'

'Just south of it, on the cliffs.'

He was a superlative thief, a cat burglar unparalleled, but when it came to a question of courage in a confrontation, he left a lot to be desired, and this suited The Growl admirably, for it made his task easier. Shooting a man in the kneecap in order to persuade him to talk is distasteful business, even if the man is wanted in at least a dozen states, dead or alive.

The Growl had no sincere hatred for Danny Bangs. 'Then it's settled. I will take over your mission for you.'

'I ain't protesting.'

'You're a wise boy, sure enough.'

The stooped man seized hold of the sack and slung it over his own saddle, but as he did so, his cowl slipped a little. This time, Danny saw more of the face of the stranger. What he had taken for white hair was actually pale fur and there was an extraordinary length to The Growl's face. Instead of a nose, the man had a snout with two snuffling nostrils.

The stranger hastily replaced the cowl and croaked a laugh, then he jumped into the saddle with amazing dexterity and saluted Danny ironically with one of his gloved hands before riding off.

Those gloves! What if they concealed paws instead of hands? Danny might have believed such a possibility, having glimpsed the countenance of The Growl and seen his eyes. The stranger was some kind of hound-man, surely! It was the worst encounter Danny had ever had.

But at least he was alive, uninjured too. If the stranger had been a werewolf or similar monster, he doubted he would be in one piece now. There was a deep mystery here, without doubt, but Danny was in no hurry to solve it. He watched the horse and rider vanish into the congealed shadows and heaved a rasping sigh of relief combined with exasperation.

Then he began walking out of the labyrinth of *Los Gigantes Rotos*, heading away from the town and away from everywhere else he was known. Time to get himself into a new place, he decided.

Augustus Strongbow sat in a saloon in Punta Arena with a beer. His patience was running out, but he still had faith in The Lord, who hadn't let him down so far. He raised the glass to his mouth with his left hand and with the index finger of his right hand he wrote formulas in the golden liquid and froth of the puddle of spilled beer on the table before him.

As a mathematician he was very good, obsessive

even, and he never felt at ease unless he was performing some calculation or other. He had done what he had been asked to do. Now he was waiting to be paid. Sending a message on the telegraph, The Lord had informed him that the money was on its way. A sack of used notes, untraceable, enough to take him wherever he wanted to go, which he supposed would be home to Canada.

Randall and Hardy had tried to discourage him from spending his free time in the town, they said it might attract too much attention to the project, but they weren't strict on this point, and so when he ignored them, they made no protest. They were fairly easy-going fellas.

The project was finished, the gun had been constructed and firmly fixed in position. It was too big and heavy to be mounted on a swivel, so it was encased in ironwork, bricks and mortar, with only the final third of the barrel protruding. The angle of elevation was one he'd worked out and couldn't be changed. That was why his abilities were so crucial.

The amount of charge needed and weight of the shell that was going to be fired was also his responsibility. The project would have been unfeasible if he'd decided not to work on it. He was the only mathematician good enough to work out the precise numbers required. And now he was here in the bar getting just a little drunk in order to pass the hours.

The propellant would be here in a day or two, his money also. Then a huge shell could be fired at the enemy, and that was that. Game over. But Strongbow knew the bluff behind the bluff. Even Randall and Hardy didn't know that Japan wasn't the true target. The port of Kesennuma had only been established a few years earlier, on June 1st, 1889 in fact.

There was no fleet being prepared there and no plans for an attack on the mainland of the USA, not now or in the near future, at any rate. Strongbow was tempted to laugh as he considered the true target. He was Canadian and had no loyalty to the United States. He was a subject of Victoria, the British queen, and his ultimate loyalty was to Britain, but he never let anyone else know this. They weren't even aware he was Canadian.

He had told them that he was from Wyoming, in order to explain away his accent, and they had swallowed this story, not being able to tell the difference. The Lord had instructed him to do this and, as always, The Lord had been right. Strongbow finished his beer and called for another and the pale barman brought the next brimming glass over to him.

'You'll be clearing out shortly, I suppose?'

Strongbow nodded.

'Yep, my work here is done.'

'And that telescope that's actually a gun. It'll be fired off soon, no doubt? I reckon the bang'll be awful.'

'Loud enough,' agreed Strongbow.

'You really think it can hit the other side of the

Pacific Ocean? I shouldn't have believed it was possible. Hit Japan and smash that one port where they're getting those ships ready to attack us?'

'Sure I do. Mister, I was the man who did the calculations, see? If it isn't all worked out to the twentieth decimal place, something might go wrong, but I worked it out to the thirty-fifth.'

The pale barman whistled. While he was whistling, the door of the saloon opened and Jeb Smith came in.

'Howdy, Frank. Give me a shot of whiskey.'

'Howdy, Jeb. Good day?'

Jeb shrugged. 'Not bad. I just been wandering around, you know, and my brain has been churning thoughts. That's what happens when you're retired and have no grandchildren to focus on.'

Frank the barman said, 'What thoughts, Jeb?'

'Just ideas churning. I say, here's one of the fellas from the telescope that ain't a telescope. How goes it, pard?'

Strongbow regarded the intrusion as unfortunate but he had nothing to hide and decided to be tolerant. 'Just fine.'

Frank spoke to Jeb, 'He says he's leaving soon.'

'Is that so?' said Jeb.

'Just waiting to get paid for the work I did,' answered Strongbow, 'and it won't be long coming, I was told.'

'The government is paying you, huh?'

'It's a government project, so yes,' said Strongbow, but now he felt just a little uneasy.

Instead of remaining quiet, he began to babble. 'Going home with my pay when I get a chance, home is in Wyoming, a little place you have never heard of, doubt I'll come back here.'

'What, you ain't gonna wait for the supergun to be fired? It's a question of defending our country. That's right, defending the good old US of A against the Empire of Japan, and you don't intend to stay and watch it? That's mighty odd, I reckon. Stoked my curiosity some.'

Strongbow was flustered. He drained his beer at a single gulp, held up the empty glass and shouted, 'What the hell is wrong with you Americans? Poking your nose into other folk's business!'

'Why, aren't *you* an American?' cried Jeb.

Strongbow shuddered.

He had been indiscreet thanks to an outburst of temper. If The Lord ever got wind of it, he would be furious. Desperately Strongbow tried to evade the consequences of his actions by pretending to be drunk. But his acting abilities were sorely deficient. 'Whadyya mean, me not an American? Of coursh I'z an American, bawn and bwed in the land of the fwee, the home of the bwave. You wanna start a fight with me, do ya?'

'Hey, calm down,' shouted Frank.

'You had too much to drink and I had too much to think,' said Jeb, but he was grinning and winking at Frank.

Strongbow rose and staggered out of the saloon.

Safe for the time being!

But he still felt sure that Jeb or Frank would say something to Randall or Hardy the next time they saw them. And those officers would probably relay the unhappy information to The Lord.

Strongbow sighed.

With luck, he would be gone by then.

The Growl slowed his horse one hour before dawn and decided to make camp in the shade of an overhang. Here, he would catch a few hours of sleep and refresh himself before resuming the journey. More importantly, his stallion would get a chance to recuperate. He had nothing but contempt for men who pushed animals too hard, who treated them without love.

He had an interesting personal history. His real name was, or had been, Bill Bones, and a decade ago he had been a newspaperman in Saint Louis. His editor was one of those men who believed in the supernatural and wanted Bill to chase every harebrained story with an occult aspect that ever came to his ears. He was obsessed with monsters and spooks.

He sent Bill to the Arizona desert to investigate reports of a flying reptile, a pterodactyl that had been seen there, and he sent him to the redwood forests to interview Bigfoot, and he sent him out East to look for a beast called a squonk, but Bill never found anything that he looked for. The only thing he found was a heap of trouble. But it was trouble that strengthened him in some ways, though it weakened him in others. It *changed* him.

His editor had somehow heard stories about a shaman in the Mojave Desert who lived in a cave. This shaman, who seemed to be nameless, wasn't entirely human. He could levitate and do all sorts of tricks that were real magic, not the sort of thing that stage conjurors did. Bill Bones was sent to find out more. The expedition was poorly planned. Bill had no real idea where the cave was and he was short of supplies for such an exploit.

He ran out of water while riding through the desert. His map was useless. His horse stumbled and broke a leg, throwing Bill, who bruised himself. It was a sad moment when he saw that he had to put his horse out of its misery and ever since, the echo of that gunshot had bounced through his skull. He staggered in an anguished daze, barely conscious of where he was, wholly ignorant of where he might be going, fully prepared for death.

At long last, as the sun was setting, he reached a rocky outcrop and lurched into a cave he found at the base of a cliff. He collapsed and fell unconscious. He was woken by nightmares, the thrashings of an injured horse with madly rolling eyes who bared long teeth at him and said, 'You have slain God,' in a voice that was horrible. Half dazed, he reached for his gun and discharged it at the unseen ceiling, where the dream images had floated. The noise of the shot was amazing and brought jagged rocks tumbling down.

The rocks missed him but the cave mouth, which had provided a faint light from the starry sky that allowed him to orient himself, was blocked. He crawled towards it and realised he was trapped, lacking the ability to shift the rocks. He plunged into unconsciousness again and welcomed this oblivion as a relief from suffering. No longer did he dream. His mind was empty, a void, a portal, a door that had been left wide open. He awoke.

In the shadows he saw a figure and he wondered if this was the shaman he had been sent to find. The only illumination came from an oil lamp spluttering in the furthest corner of the cave. He sat up and then his mouth gaped, for now he could discern the features of the figure who occupied the cave. It was a face that strongly resembled that of a wolf or a dog. It wasn't human. And yet there was something wise about its expression.

Whether this was the shaman his editor had told him about, or some other shaman, seemed irrelevant to him at that moment. And indeed, he was never to learn the answer to that question. The only thing that concerned him was that he was trapped without food or water in a cave with a creature that was half-dog at least and for sure it might not be friendly.

His worries were unnecessary. The figure spoke and told him not to fear. It had a soothing voice despite the fact it often lapsed into short sharp barks. Bill allowed himself to be reassured by the words of this being, who spoke English with many

Spanish words thrown in and some other words that surely were of indigenous origin. Bill guessed the meaning of the words he didn't know thanks to their context. He listened and nodded.

The shaman told him that there was a way to escape the sealed cave but the way had a price. Bill would have to learn some of the magic the shaman could teach, but the process involved certain transformations in the pupil's mind. And a modification of the mind is often reflected in changes of the body. This was the choice Bill was given. Death from thirst in the cave or semi-shaman status. He unhesitatingly opted for training in magic.

The ordeal began. Bill learned to focus his mind so fiercely that the normal limitations of human thought were surpassed. Astounding ideas galloped around in his brain at breakneck speed and he achieved a strange clarity of inner vision that threatened to overwhelm him with new perspectives and interpretations. He deepened his appreciation of abstractions.

Greater control over his mind and nervous system enabled him to survive a difficulty that ordinarily would have finished him in a few days. He reduced his need for water and food to a minimum, so that the few drops of moisture on the cave walls, licked off with his tongue, were enough to sustain him and a handful of dried herbs the shaman gave him from a pouch once a week was sufficient to satisfy his hunger. He was an able student.

At the same time, he felt the change in his body, the reshaping of his form. He was becoming more and more doglike, his hands turning into paws, his face into a long snout, his tongue much thicker and longer. At last his teacher called to him through the gloom, 'You are ready,' and he truly felt he was. Six months had passed since he first entered the cave.

'Master, should I try to clear the blockage with the power of my mind?' he asked, and the shaman shook his head.

'With the increased strength of my new limbs?' cried Bill, but the shaman still replied in the negative. 'Then how?'

The shaman barked a laugh. 'There is a second entrance to this cave. Why do you think I was so unperturbed by the rockfall that sealed us in? You never asked me about another entrance. You had already decided you were trapped in here, that there was only one exit. But to find this alternative opening, you must venture down a labyrinth of passages.'

'Labyrinth? Then I stand a chance of becoming lost?'

'A human would perish.'

'Am I not human now, master?' asked Bill.

'Rather less than before.'

'May I take the oil lamp with me? The oil lamp that never seems to need to be refilled with oil but burns forever?'

'No, Bill, for that is mine and I require it.'

'Then how shall I navigate?'

'Use your nose, your superior sense of smell. Sniff out the route along the dark passages underground. Rely on your canine qualities, not your human. All logic will betray you, so employ instinct.'

And he raised a paw in farewell and moved from the spot he had occupied since first introducing himself to Bill, and now Bill saw what the shaman's body had been concealing all this time, a small opening in the back wall of the cave that led to the maze of narrow passages.

Bill licked his lips and his chin. 'I still don't know your name. May I know what you are rightly called, master?'

The shaman considered this request. He said at last, 'Dogface is what the people of my tribe would call me. It is good enough.' He paused again and then he grinned. 'But you may call me Tony.' His paw was still lifted high and with closed eyes he lifted it higher and howled.

Bill allowed the howl to fill his soul. Dogface was singing the wild song of the cursed moon, the song of the ancient night, the song of the lonely desert, the song of the dreaming cactus, the song of the sky father and earth mother, a song of the tumbleweed and drifting dust.

Bill listened carefully, with a sombre joy and a deep respect. He was only a semi-shaman, maybe not even that, but already he had altered his beliefs to such a degree that he felt fully reborn.

He raised his own paw in acknowledgement.

Then he began his escape.

It was like birth in reverse, he felt, as he squeezed himself into that conduit and writhed his way along it. The passages diverged, a whole cosmos of tangled ways presented itself to him, and he was acutely aware that if he took the wrong turning at any point, he would never emerge again. He would be entombed, and even his improved stamina wouldn't save him, for he wasn't able to exist on *no* food or water. He wasn't an immortal.

Snuffling, his nose working ceaselessly, he smelt the fresh air of the desert beyond the walls of rock. He followed his nose. Frequently the narrower route was the one he took, although his reason rebelled against it, but his nose had the final word, the upper hand, the guiding nostril. He obeyed it. Among the skills he had learned from the shaman was humility, the ability to ignore the lies of the ego, the deceptions of the waking self.

An hour passed, two, and finally he saw a glimmer of light ahead. With the quiet determination of a geological process he inched himself down the passage that disgorged him at the base of the rocky outcrop which held the cave, but on the far side. This passage was an extremely tight fit and he was bruised when he emerged in the pale pre-dawn light. Much of his fur had been rubbed off during the ordeal and it would never regrow.

Bill Bones blinked at the lightening sky and laughed. He was Bill no more. A low growl emerged from his throat.

He was The Growl and that's how he liked it.

Although he was thousands of miles away, The Lord also had an interesting personal history. He was a direct descendant of Major-General Sir Isaac Brock, a British hero of the 1812 war against the United States of America. Brock had excelled in campaigns against his enemies, had invaded the USA from Canada and captured Fort Detroit. His successes continued, but he was killed in combat at the Battle of Queenston Heights on 13th October of that year. The battle was decisively won by the British nonetheless.

Almost two years later, a large British force under Major General Robert Ross entered Washington and burned down the White House. The war came to an end shortly afterwards, but there was a messy climax, for neither side could sincerely declare that they had won. Yet it wasn't a stalemate. Technically, the British triumphed, for they had defended Canada and all their other possessions in North America. But the citizens of the United States had acquired an even deeper appreciation of their independence.

Relations between the two nations remained peaceful afterwards, but this wasn't good enough for The Lord. He rankled on behalf of his dead ancestor, a fierce flame of hatred burned inside him. On the surface he was suave, cultured and indifferent, but deep down he raged and foamed at the injustices of history. The White House had been destroyed, yes, but it had been rebuilt since, and he regarded that as an insult to the British Empire, to the men who had been killed in that unusual war, and to his family name.

The Lord craved revenge. Although he personally shouldn't have a grudge against the Americans, he was driven by an atavistic zeal that he justified as an expression of pure patriotism, a relentless obsession with destroying the White House *again*, and this time comprehensively. He would smash it so thoroughly that nobody would ever try rebuilding it. He sounded out his friends on the idea and they rejected it. This made him still more furious and determined. He made a nuisance of himself, petitioning Members of Parliament to declare war on the United States, always agitating for action.

He was ignored by the peerage, who regarded him as a lunatic, until at last they were no longer able to ignore him. He was exiled from their society and he was shunned by the nobility whose members he had previously counted as close friends. Driven even madder by this neglect, he abandoned Britain in his yacht, *The Bounder*, and found himself a new home in Spain, where notions of empire and vengeance still went hand in hand.

It was during the ascension of the new king Amadeo, after decades of acute turmoil, that The Lord established himself in the port town of

Tarragona on the Mediterranean coast. He bought a pleasant villa, though he practically lived on his yacht, which was anchored offshore.

But he often pulled up the anchor and sailed far and wide, searching for allies and distractions. His dream of teaching the Americans a lesson had no firm basis in reality. All he knew was that the White House must be obliterated, turned into atoms that would drift away on the wind, and that the site where it had stood should become a crater.

On one of his journeys to Canada, where he often went, regarding it as a bulwark against northward expansion by the USA, he happened by chance to meet the engineer and mathematician Augustus Strongbow in a dining room in a hotel in Montreal. Strongbow was also the descendant of a man killed in the 1812 war, an artillery expert. They began talking and a really outrageous idea began to form in The Lord's mind.

A colossal cannon, a supergun powerful enough to hit the White House. But if it was located in Canada, that would incite war and Canada would lose. Therefore the gun must be located on American soil. But how? Would he ever be able to hire American workers willing to construct a gun that pointed at an American target? It seemed implausible. So the workers must be tricked. He knew a way in which this could be done.

After the engineer heard The Lord's idea, his fertile mind began working on the problem. Strongbow was confident he could design a workable supergun with an almost limitless range. The Lord knew that he wouldn't be able to hire any American citizens, no matter how criminally minded they were, to work on such a project, so he constructed an elaborate ruse. He would claim that he was building the supergun in order to sink an enemy fleet that was being readied in the Japanese port of Kesennuma.

If the gun pointed inland, the labourers would refuse to build it, yes, but if it was pointing at the ocean, they would assume The Lord was telling the truth about wanting to defend the USA from a Japanese fleet. In fact, this supergun would be powerful enough to project a shell right around the world and destroy the White House from an easterly direction. But only The Lord and Strongbow knew this. The location of the supergun would be on American soil on the same latitude as the White House, 38.8977°N.

Strongbow next calculated the precise amount of propellant needed in the gun to score a direct hit on the White House. Who would suspect a gun on the California coast pointing away from the USA? No one! The Lord would return to Tarragona and communicate with Strongbow via telegraph. He would also arrange to hire two reliable officers who, in turn, would hire the labourers. He would control everything by telegraph. The Lord absolutely refused to set foot on American soil. It was anathema to him.

Events proceeded smoothly enough. An

extremely large dent was made in The Lord's fortunes, but he consoled himself that an even bigger dent would be made in the earth of Washington once he was done. He hired Randall and Hardy, paid for men and materials, kept his identity and location a mystery, cultivated the clever rumour that he was working for the American government and that Japan was the necessary target.

And when his finances ran very low, he had the initiative to turn to crime to secure more funds, hiring Danny Bangs to rob banks in order to pay the men who worked for him, Strongbow included. Strongbow's payment was the final one, as it happened, and the moment it was delivered and Strongbow confirmed he had received it, The Lord would issue instructions to fire the gun. Strongbow didn't want to hang around for that event.

His caution was sensible. He wanted as little evidence of his involvement as possible. Randall or Hardy would pull the trigger, innocently enough, under the impression they were launching a pre-emptive strike on an invasion fleet on the far side of the Pacific, rather than launching a projectile into a sub-orbit that would encircle the majority of the planet's circumference and come down white hot with vastly accumulated energy smack on top of their own government's headquarters and blow it to tiny pieces.

The engineer disliked the Americans for what they'd done to his unlucky ancestor, and he loved

Canada and therefore the British Empire, and he wanted revenge almost as much as The Lord did. But he wasn't quite as single-minded in his quest to get even. He wasn't a fanatic. He sat on a chair in his quarters, a frown on his forehead, and he hoped that his payment would arrive tomorrow. He had already embarrassed himself in front of Frank and Jeb and he supposed he might make things worse if he hung around Punta Arena much longer. Time to be long gone. Hurry up, Danny Bangs!

Danny would never meet Strongbow but Strongbow wouldn't become aware of this fact until it was too late. The Growl awoke refreshed after his brief sleep in the shelter of an overhang. It was still night, stars burned without twinkling, nor did his eyes twinkle as he regarded them. His horse was well-rested too and he mounted it with a single bound.

The Growl jerked the reins and was off. But he hadn't ridden more than a mile before his acute hearing told him something was wrong. The faint rustle of cloth, the distinct click of a lever-action Winchester. He could have spurred his horse faster but he preferred to slow down. The barrel of the rifle poked at him from between two tumbled rocks.

'Easy now,' the muffled voice said, and The Growl knew at once that he faced no ordinary outlaw. He replied:

'Can't get no easier than me. Easiest of all, I am.'

'Good. But no tricks!'

The Growl walked his horse closer.

'That's far enough!' cried the voice. 'Stop right there. Remove that cowl, pard. Let's have a good look at you.'

The cowl was swept back. The head of The Growl thrust itself forward, a truly startling sight, especially at night. There was a sharp intake of breath and this was followed by a short laugh.

'Should I call you Rover or Spot or Patch?'

'I am The Growl.'

'Really? How's about that then?'

'And *your* name?'

'Don't mind giving it to you. Jalamity Kane. Seeing as we ain't properly acquainted yet, I reckon it's best if you just call me Kane. I don't like being on first name terms with those I gotta kill. Makes the job harder, you see. Not that I am a sentimental kind of person.'

'Kane's a mighty strange name for a gal.'

'How did you know?'

'That you are a gal? My senses are pretty keen. Men and women give off different auras and yours has more of a feminine colour to it, but it's not exactly what I'd call womanly for all that, you know. Auras aren't just shimmers of hue but contain patterns that aren't always abstract. Men's auras are full of shapes that look like nails and hammers, guns and knives, while women's auras burst with the forms of curtains and cushions, ribbons and corsets. I see furnishings in *your* aura, but I also see bullets.'

This observation was greeted with a shrug.

'Magic man, are you?'

'I have a certain number of limited powers.'

'Me too, funnily enough. Now let me ask you a question, cos it's my turn. I want to know something real bad.'

'Ask me anything.'

'What kind of aura does a *dog* have?'

The Growl snorted at this.

'Touché,' he cried.

'What kinda lingo is that? You a Frenchie?'

The Growl snorted again.

'Why don't we get down to business? You clearly aren't intending to rob me, which is ironic considering how this is one of the very few occasions when I might be worth robbing. You seem more keen to kill me. So why don't you get on with the job? Why the delay?'

Jalamity Kane pursed her lips and answered:

'I want you to *know*.'

'Know what? Why you want to kill me? You said yourself that we'd never met before, so it can't be on account of any old grudge. Reckon there's a hatred inside you that ain't my doing.'

'Pard, you're right, and I'll tell you. I am hunting all the men who are part animal. I know what it means that you're a man-dog, it means you studied with a shaman, one of the Mojave wizards. When I was younger and full of hope and desire, I too sought out a shaman to study with. I found one. Seven years in the depths of the ground, in a subterranean cavern, putting myself through horrible exercises, expanding my mind! But it didn't work, I didn't acquire the power. I failed and my soul became bitter.'

The Growl now regarded her with a measure of sympathy. But she sneered at the kindness in his eyes. 'I vowed,' she continued, 'to destroy those who had succeeded. I hunt them down. The cat-men, racoon-men, eagle-men, snake-men and yes, the dog-men too. Hunt them down and kill them. That's my mission in life. I have no interest in money.'

The Growl said, 'Did you learn nothing in seven years? Didn't a change of *any* kind take place inside you?'

'My shaman told me I hadn't failed, in fact he said I had succeeded, But it was the kind of animal I became that distressed me. That's why I regard myself as a failure. You became part dog. I became part man. A man is an animal too, I was told. But it's not good enough!'

Jalamity Kane stepped out from behind the rocks.

The Growl whistled low.

He saw an attractive woman with the stance of a man. Her face was oval, a pleasant outline under a mane of wild hair, her eyelashes were long, her lips an alluring shape, but her body was muscular and taut, her shoulders wide, and her attitude was one of simmering aggression. Her finger was on the trigger of her Winchester. He had only a few moments left to take action. Remembering what Danny had done to him, he decided to do the same to this stranger. He grabbed the bulging sack of money and flung it.

She loosed off a shot that was blocked by the flying sack, and some of the bank notes inside ended up with holes through them, but the force of the bullet was reduced so dramatically by this buffer that when it struck The Growl in the chest it only broke the topmost layer of his skin through his shirt before falling harmlessly to the ground. He howled.

His howl was triumphant but not merciless.

The sack struck her squarely.

It toppled her over. Down she went, sprawling, the Winchester knocked out of her grip. The Growl galloped forwards, leaned out of the saddle to snatch up the sack, then he was off into the darkness at full speed. By the time she realised what had happened, it was too late to fire again at him. He was out of range and with a curse she shook her fist at the shadows that concealed his fleeing back. It was one of the few times a potential victim had escaped her and her chagrin was considerable, though mixed with respect.

'That was well played,' she said to herself, 'but speed and surprise won't save him forever. I'll catch up with him one day. The Growl, eh? I'll remember that name. He might not know it, but every dog has his day. His day will come, sure enough. No one escapes in the end.'

No one escapes in the end. Those words could have been the motto of Randall and Hardy as they sat in their shack and debated what had happened. The rider had approached just before noon. He had knocked at their door and asked for the whereabouts of Mr Strongbow.

'And why exactly would you be wanting to inquire after him?' Randall asked, pleasantly enough, but with a significant glance at Hardy. The newcomer replied with equal politeness.

'I have official business to discuss.'

'Would you be so kind as to state your identity?'

'Danny Bangs,' said The Growl.

Randall and Hardy exchanged another glance. 'Ah, to be sure. We were informed that you were coming.'

'The Lord gave me strict instructions.'

Randall thought to himself, 'Yes, I know, in fact I am the one who passed on his instructions to you, but you don't look anything like the fella who went off to rob a bank'. But his face remained bland. He gave away nothing, neither did Hardy. Both kept up the pretence.

'I am looking for Augustus Strongbow.'

'You already told us that, friend. Why don't you come inside and sit down and we will send for that man?'

'My mission is urgent. I prefer to seek him out myself. If you would reveal where he currently is, I'll be going.'

Something in the voice of this impostor made Randall hesitate. There were hints of menace in it. He licked his lips. Hardy was of a like mind, for he leaned forward and said, 'He's probably in Punta

Arena. We haven't seen much of him lately. He spends a lot of time in the saloons there. He is waiting for you, full of beer, very impatient. That's all.'

He was eager to get rid of the stranger.

The Growl nodded once and left the shack. They stood at the window and watched him riding northwards to the town. On the clifftop path, he looked like a strange angel rather than a man, a mutant centaur, some mythic entity anyway and Randall shook his head at the sight.

'An impostor, but where does he come from?'

'The Lord told us that our government is divided on the issue of launching a strike on Japan. The department that arranged the building of the supergun is keeping it secret from the other departments. I reckon this fella is from one of those other departments. Maybe they just cottoned on and sent him to poke his nose into our business. That's my view.'

Randall and Hardy wasted no time before sending a message to The Lord, but an hour passed before the stock ticker on a desk in the corner chattered and ticker tape spilled out of the device. This was The Lord's reply. Hardy moved swiftly to snatch it up and read it as it was being printed. He glanced at Randall and said, 'Yes, he thinks the stranger is a government inspector in disguise and he asks us to treat him courteously.'

'Courteously? That's unlike The Lord's style.'

'Well, he adds that we should feel free to kidnap

and murder him if things seem about to get out of control.'

Randall pondered this and delivered his verdict. He stated cryptically, 'No one escapes in the end but the end has already gone,' and when Hardy frowned at this declaration, he laughed and added, 'The propellant shipment arrived last night. This impostor had a sack that bulged with what could have been genuine money, but even if it isn't, so what?'

Hardy said, 'It was real money. I have a nose for it.'

'So you do, my old friend.'

Hardy added, 'That Strongbow fella means nothing to us. Nor does Danny. I only care about myself and you.'

'Exactly! We were paid by The Lord to do a job and that job happens to be defending the USA against Japan. We just need Strongbow to prime the gun. It is a shame only he knows how to do that, but he designed the thing, after all. I can't see the government inspector, if that's what he is, arresting him today. He needs to gather evidence first. That will take a few days at least. I don't think it will be necessary to kidnap him.'

'I'm glad about that because I sure don't relish the idea of murdering one of our own side's secret agents.'

'Nor me. But you know something, our government won't always do what is good for the country. So we have to take matters into our own hands. Blow up that fleet in Kesennuma, I mean.'

'I am just as determined as you are.'

'As soon as the imposter pays Strongbow, whether with real banknotes or counterfeit ones, the engineer will come to prime the gun. Then we shall fire it and destroy the enemy fleet. *Then* we'll get the hell out of here. History will be our judges and will judge us kindly.'

They hadn't budged but stood by the window, watching the figure of The Growl on his horse shrink to a dot. The shadow of the supergun reminded them that shortly the deadly shell would be blasted at a muzzle velocity greater than 1000 m/s. The enemies of the United States would be only five and a half hours away from learning a very harsh lesson.

The door of the saloon opened. The Growl entered and looked around. Standing behind the bar, Frank looked up. Seated at the bar, Jeb also looked up. Nobody said anything as the stooped man in the cowl waved aside Frank's silent offer of a glass of beer and peered into the corners of the room. A sawdust sprinkled floor, vacant chairs and tables, a billiard table with torn baize and warped cues. The place was empty. The Growl was disappointed.

'Is this the only saloon in town?'

'Nope,' said Frank, 'but it's the most popular.'

The Growl studied the lifeless room with an ironic smile on his shadowed mouth. Then he said thickly:

'I'm looking for a man named Strongbow.'

'We know of him.'

'He's not here, obviously.'

'He don't come here much anymore. I suppose he's in his hotel room. It's the only hotel in Punta Arena.'

The Growl nodded his thanks and left. Jeb spat on the boards. 'Did you see his face under that cowl? Looked just like a dog I used to own. Ridgeback, nice dog, loyal and noble. Kept getting fleas and ticks, though. Used to walk all day with that dog, miles and miles. Made this funny little sound when you tickled his belly. Real strange sound, it was.'

'What kind of sound?' Frank wanted to know.

'It was a sort of "whoo whee yeee yoo". Can't rightly get the accent right. It sort of slid up and down a scale, a glissando. That's the correct term for it, I think? I mean, most dogs howl and whine, but mine was more melodic, like he was rehearsing for a concert, but only when you tickled him. On the belly. That dog was a man's best pal, surely.'

'That stranger just now. He looked like your dog?'

'Spitting image,' said Jeb.

'Now that's curious,' Frank opined. They stared at the door through which The Growl had departed. His horse was still tethered outside but they didn't care about that. They were thinking about the tall tales they had heard in their youth, the campfire stories about werewolves and coyote-men and shapeshifters, tales they didn't believe but didn't think were lies either. Stories that must be listened to without forming a definite opinion.

They puffed out their cheeks as they remembered.

Then they drank their beer.

Meanwhile, the Growl was prowling the streets. He prowled until he found the hotel. He entered, walked past the alarmed receptionist without even looking at him, went up the rickety stairs, threw off his cowl with a flick of his wrist and twitched his abnormally long ears. He was listening and sniffing, his inhuman senses alert, his thick tongue lolling.

Finally he worked out which door to knock on. He rapped and waited and receiving no answer, he tried turning the handle. The door was locked. Now he growled and shouldered the door off its hinges. The door fell into the room and Augustus Strongbow jumped off the bed, where he had been snoozing. His face was creased and his eyes blinked.

'Are you from The Lord? Are you here to punish me because I revealed that I'm Canadian? What'll you do?'

The Growl realised Strongbow had unwittingly given him an advantage and he decided to employ it. In the long run, it would lessen the need for any form of violence. So he nodded.

'Scared of The Lord, are you, pal?'

Strongbow gulped.

The Growl said, 'If you do what I say, there'll be no need for you to ever fear him again. But first I want you to talk. Now bear something in mind. I'm a nice fella, I don't like suffering of any kind, but I have special talents, and one of these talents is that I *tend* to know when someone is lying or telling the truth, and so I'm asking you politely to tell me the truth. Seems to me that you have a choice. The Lord or me. I'm sure you would rather not deal with either of us. I am sorry to say that option doesn't exist.'

'The Lord or you?'

The Growl nodded. 'Tell me.'

'Tell you? Everything, you mean? But I only ever wanted to get paid and go home. Yes, I was motivated by revenge, but it was never a big issue for me, not like it was for The Lord.'

'Start at the beginning,' said The Growl.

'You won't hurt me?'

'I give you my word, pard.'

Strongbow nodded meekly. He sat down on the edge of the bed. His eyes were bloodshot, his hands shook, but his voice was clear. He related all that he knew, which was pretty much everything important, and when he finished, The Growl felt he knew The Lord well. He also felt he knew Strongbow well. While he considered what to do next, the engineer rose from the bed, took the sack of cash that The Growl had put down on the floor, clutched it close to his chest and made his way gingerly to the door.

He reached for the handle and The Growl asked, 'Where are you going? I think that's bad manners, friend.'

'I did what you asked. I told you everything. You said you hated suffering, so I reckon you ain't going to torture me. I think I have earned the right to leave now. I was waiting for the money.'

'Your ordeal isn't over yet, I'm afraid.'

'But I don't care about the White House! Don't you get it? It's something I would like to see destroyed, but if that doesn't happen I ain't too bothered. I am no fanatic. Just let me go, willya?'

'Remain where you are. Don't move.'

'You promised you wouldn't hurt me. You gave me your word. So what is to stop me just leaving the room and the hotel and getting out of Punta Arena? I don't feel welcome here no more.'

The Growl threw back his head and howled.

It was a howl that sounded like an ancient curse, a long drawn-out cry of rage and horror. Strongbow was aghast.

'What the hell was that?'

'My word,' said The Growl menacingly. 'I gave it to you and now you've finished with it, I'm taking it back.'

'Wait!' cried Strongbow. He threw up his hands in surrender, dropping the sack of money as he did so. 'Please!'

'I am going to sit on your bed and devise a plan. I want you to be quiet and not try any funny business. Then we'll leave together. I really don't want to hurt you, but I will if it proves necessary.'

Strongbow slumped to the floor and curled up into a ball. He sucked at his thumb and clamped his eyelids tight.

The Growl sat and created his plan. Then it was time to put his plan into action. He stood and nudged Strongbow with the toe of his boot. The engineer uncurled himself and stood unsteadily. The Growl opened the door and ushered him into the corridor. They went down the rickety stairway together and at the bottom the receptionist confronted them across his desk. He was fiddling with a shotgun, a crude but powerful double-barrelled weapon. He was having a problem loading it and the sweat poured from his face.

'I summoned the sheriff and he'll be coming soon. I sent a messenger boy to fetch him. Can't have intruders breaking into this hotel. What are you doing with that resident? Abducting him!'

The Growl stepped forward and licked the face of the receptionist, his long crimson tongue rasping the astonished features of the fellow. Then he turned on his heel and hustled Strongbow towards the exit. The receptionist was clutching at his face, trying to pull off the strings of drool. He had dropped his gun and he was screaming as he battled the slobber.

With the hotel behind them, The Growl returned to the saloon for his horse and he walked it to where

Strongbow had left his own horse, which was in one of the stables on the south side of town.

'Don't try anything foolish,' warned The Growl.

Strongbow smiled nervously.

'I know you ain't no fool,' continued The Growl, 'and in fact you happen to be a genius, dontcha? The problem is that geniuses often don't know what is best for themselves. They are cute when it comes to equations and outer space and all that kind of stuff. But when it comes to preserving their own hides, they have a tendency to be a little mad.'

'I'm as sane as they come,' said Strongbow.

'Glad to hear that.'

They rode together towards the supergun.

Along the clifftop path they went and while they did so, The Growl gave a set of instructions to the engineer.

He explained his plan and he made sure that Strongbow was aware of what would happen to him if he didn't go along with it. But for the engineer, it wasn't a big deal who prevailed in the end, The Lord or The Growl. At the moment, it was The Growl who had the upper hand, or paw, and that was fine by him. The obliteration of the White House would have been deeply satisfying, but he could live without it. He listened carefully.

The Growl asked him:

'There's no way of adjusting the angle of the supergun, I take it? I thought not. What about lessening the mass of the shell? That's out of the question too? Too tricky a task. Fine, there's a third option. I want the shell to land where The Lord isn't expecting it to strike, see?'

'The third option?'

The Growl informed the engineer that he was required to adjust the amount of charge in the supergun, reducing it by a precise percentage. The Growl didn't know what this percentage should be. He was relying on Strongbow to do all the calculations properly, without cheating.

The Growl said that his unnatural senses would let him know if Strongbow tried to be dishonest in his calculations. The engineer believed him. He had no intention of sabotaging The Growl's plan. He was too intimidated for that. The best thing to do was to be obedient.

They reached the site of the gun and approached the shack where Randall and Hardy were quartered. The controls for the gun were located here too. The Growl made sure his cowl was firmly in place, then he dismounted. Strongbow also dismounted. The door to the shack opened. Randall had been standing at the window, watching and waiting.

'I found him,' said The Growl cheerfully.

'Can see that. And so?'

'Our business was concluded amiably. Now he wants to do what he has to do with the supergun. Prime it.'

'And fire it? And blast the Japanese fleet into nothingness? Well, we have been waiting patiently for this day.'

He invited them inside. Strongbow made for the nearest desk and took pen and paper and began on the calculations. The Growl just stood there. Randall was a little aloof at first, then he exchanged a meaningful glance with Hardy and said in a friendly manner, 'I don't believe you have told us your name. It would be nice for us to know who we have the honour of addressing. I don't like being in a room with an unknown stranger.'

'I already told you. Danny Bangs,' said The Growl, but he hesitated for a moment and Randall nodded.

'Of course! How could I have forgotten?'

Randall stepped casually to one of the other desks and opened a drawer. He fumbled inside it for a moment. He was searching for something among all the clutter that had gathered there since the project was initiated. Papers rustled and pencils rattled and then finally he found what he wanted. There was a click and a smooth sound of the closing drawer.

Then he whirled around and pointed his revolver at The Growl. 'Not good enough. Time to find out who you really are and what you really want. Remove that cowl for a start and then you –'

Before he could say more, The Growl had launched himself at Randall. He moved so fast, Randall was unable to squeeze the trigger in time. The collision knocked Randall against the wall of the shack. His head struck a nail embedded in the wall with such force that his skull split. He rebounded to the middle of the room and that is where his skull broke wide open and his brain flopped onto the floor. Hardy was on his feet and running at The Growl but he hadn't noticed the steaming mess on the bare boards.

He skidded in the gunk, lost his balance and came down hard on the brain on his rump. The brain was compressed under his weight and burst, spraying a multitude of thick jets in all directions. Hardy was appalled and he desperately yearned to blame someone for this atrocious mishap. It was Randall's tumbled body that he turned to when he said:

'That's another fine mess you've got me into!'

Then he wept, both for himself and his friend, his tears mingling with the grey, red and yellow ooze of Randall.

This mess *wasn't* fine.

Despite the trauma of the event, The Growl was busy with the telegraph in the corner. He was messaging The Lord, pretending to be Strongbow as he did so. First he explained that Randall and Hardy were both unwell, they might even have typhoid, so they had taken to their beds, just one bed actually, but who was he to offer any judgement? He was an engineer, that's all. He only prayed they would recover, but who could say?

Then he went on to state that he, Strongbow, had taken over the running of the project. His money had been delivered by Danny and because he was safely alone in the operating room of the shack, out of earshot, he could be forthright about the true target of the supergun.

He was looking forward to destroying the White House. The shell would be like a divine bolt of energy. A beautiful sight as it left the barrel of the gun on its journey around most of the world.

The next part of his message to The Lord was a suggestion about sailing his yacht out of the port of Tarragona and to a position where he could witness the shell flying overhead like a beautiful meteor. He thought The Lord ought to treat himself to all the fruits of victory. Why only read about the pulverising of the White House in a newspaper? Why not see with his own eyes the burning missile that would cause the smash?

The suggested position was a point on the Mediterranean Sea close to Es Vedrà, a rocky islet southwest of the Spanish island of Ibiza. The Growl knew maps by heart, it was another of his uncanny abilities, and now his knowledge came in useful. Still playing the part of Strongbow, he detailed how wondrous and inspiring the sight would be of the blazing shell passing above The Lord's yacht on its way to the seat of government of the United States, a country that by rights ought to belong to Britain.

He sat back and waited for The Lord to respond. In the meantime, Hardy was recovering and Strongbow had finished his calculations. The Growl asked the engineer to find some rope or cord and tie Hardy tight. While this tying up was taking place, the stock ticker started chattering. The Growl read the ticker tape as it came out of the machine.

'He's fallen for it. He's swallowed the ruse.'

Strongbow nodded.

'He is setting sail immediately,' said The Growl, 'so now I want you to do more calculations. You must work out how long it will take the airborne shell to reach a certain longitude. Timing is of the essence here. The Lord will reach the coordinates I have given him, which are 38.8977°N, 1.208°E, in twenty hours or so. Work it out properly! I want the shell to land at that precise point when The Lord is anchored there. Understand?'

Augustus Strongbow licked his trembling lips.

Quentin Brock, also known as The Lord, at least to himself and his associates, breathed deeply as he stood on the deck of *The Bounder* and inhaled the pure clean air of the sea. His yacht was a magnificent vessel, sleek, painted a deep blue colour with red and white stripes. The sails billowed and the craft was a joy to behold as it skimmed the waves.

'Soon those rascally rebels in the American colonies will be punished in a manner most suitable!' he yelled to his crew of three loyal retainers and the few gulls that kept pace with his vessel.

He had left Tarragona more than a dozen hours earlier, after receiving that message from Strongbow, and now he checked his position with a sextant. Yes, they would be approaching Ibiza before too long and then veering to anchor a mile or so offshore of Es Vedrà, an uninhabited islet.

It was necessary for him to be on the same latitude as the shell to witness it at its most gorgeous, the same latitude as the supergun and the White House and also the Japanese port that stood in for a decoy. He wondered about Randall and Hardy. How would they feel when they recovered from typhoid and learned that they had unwittingly aided the devastating attack on their own government? He almost winced as he thought about it.

But maybe they wouldn't recover. That would be best for all. Putting down his qualms, he shouted in utter glee.

'The scoundrels of America, those traitors and blighters, are going to wish they had remained loyal to the crown!'

He hoped Strongbow would wait to pull the trigger until he was properly anchored in the assigned spot. On second thoughts, there would be a delay as the shell flew across the Pacific Ocean, the entirety of the continent of Asia, the width of the continent of Europe, and then the Atlantic Ocean before striking its target like a divine clenched fist full of thunderbolts. More spectacular than any comet, he supposed the sight would be.

How long would that delay be? Ten hours? Who knew! Only Strongbow could be relied upon to work it out and take the delay into account. He would pull the trigger at the right time. The Lord would be in position when it passed overhead. That's all that mattered. He had a bottle of Champagne ready for the occasion. Everything would be perfect.

He was unaware that Strongbow was waiting with two other persons, one of them bound tightly with a cord, the other sitting on a chair with his tongue hanging out. Hardy made no attempt to struggle and this was wise. The Growl made no attempt to hide his face. His cowl was thrown back and the *doggedness* of his appearance was plain to view.

There was a pocket watch on the desk nearest him.

Now and then, he glanced at it from the corner of his vision and at long last he turned to the engineer. 'Are you *certain* you loaded the gun with the correct amount of charge? No more, no less?'

Strongbow nodded. The Growl stared at him.

'I believe you,' he said.

The engineer arched his eyebrows.

'Pull the trigger,' said The Growl very quietly.

Strongbow went over to a console. The trigger of the supergun bore almost no resemblance to the trigger of a normal gun. There was a trigger guard but the trigger itself was a row of buttons.

Strongbow lifted off the guard and pressed the buttons in sequence. There was a delay as the relays worked.

The trigger mechanism was electro-mechanical.

At last the primer was activated. The chemical reaction began. The initiator and the sensitiser ignited, and then fuel caught, sustaining the produced flame to enable the main charge to combust.

The explosion followed and the shack fell apart.

The supergun erupted.

The Growl was flung to the floor and so was Strongbow. Hardy, who was already seated on the floor, was flung upright. The wooden debris settled around them, splinters jabbing them in sensitive places. Hardy tried to make his escape by hopping but was so dazed by the blast he fell over and knocked himself out. The Growl recovered before Strongbow.

He stood, his ears ringing, his body throbbing.

'Incredible!' he gasped.

In Punta Arena, all the windows had shattered. Frank and Jeb regarded the broken glasses they were holding.

'Reckon that's the end of the Japanese fleet.'

'They owe us for the beer!'

'I'll drink to that.'

'Me too. But *how*, for crying out loud?'

They sighed and staggered out of the saloon into the streets. They were in time to witness the blazing meteor vanishing over the horizon. But it was still climbing. Frank frowned and said, 'I ain't no ballistics expert, but that angle is a little too steep. Seems that way to me.'

'What do you mean?' cried Jeb and he glowered

at it. 'Are you saying it's going to miss that fleet in Kesennuma and that the Japanese will still be able to invade us? Bad shot, is that the case?'

'Reckon it's going to overshoot Japan, I do.'

'So we're doomed then?'

'We'd better learn to like sushi just in case.'

'What's sushi?' cried Jeb.

'Dunno, just heard some sailors talking about it. Some kind of music style I reckon, like bluegrass banjos.'

'But it's not actually banjos, is it?'

'Nope. Can't be.'

Jeb frowned. 'Wonder what it sounds like?'

'Perhaps like this …'

Frank thrummed his lips, making a strange twanging noise. The blast had disordered his senses a little and he didn't really know what he was doing. Jeb listened politely to this mouth music but shook his head after a minute and said bluntly, 'Don't think that's right.'

'Probably not,' agreed Frank sadly.

The Lord had reached his destination in *The Bounder* and the vessel was riding at anchor. The islet of Es Vedrà loomed near. He was lying on the deck, staring up at the sky. The projectile would pass directly overhead, fizzing and whizzing like a phosphorus cricket ball.

He liked receiving joy on his back. It was the most satisfying position for it and he hummed to himself as he waited. Then one of his retainers shouted and he turned his head. The meteor was rising in the east, climbing over the horizon and it was even more beautiful than he had expected it to be. Bright white, yes, but speckled with pale green.

'Say farewell to the White House!'

He held up a brimming glass of Champagne. But the bubbles were few and far between in the liquid now.

He had ordered the bottle to be opened prematurely, but no matter. It was a gesture, nothing more. He didn't even like Champagne. He was toasting the sky and the doom soaring through it.

Strangely, the projectile stopped climbing. It levelled off. The Lord didn't worry too much about this. Strongbow had made the calculations, therefore they must be correct. He was one of the great mathematicians of the age they lived in and a loyal subject of the British Empire.

The Lord laughed.

And he was still laughing when the projectile began its descent. The Lord's confidence in Strongbow's mathematical skills was slightly misplaced, for the calculations contained a small error.

Instead of hitting the yacht, the incoming shell struck the islet of Es Vedrà and blew off a massive chunk of it.

And it was this chunk that landed on *The Bounder* and effortlessly sunk it, together with The Lord and his three retainers. No wreckage longer than an inch remained floating on the oily surface.

The Lord's confidence in Strongbow's patriotism was *very* misplaced, for the engineer was one of those men who loved themselves more than their flag and that quality was the key to his present survival. The Growl released him and even allowed him to keep one third of Danny's money. 'I will keep one third for myself,' he told the engineer.

'The final third? What about that?'

The Growl shrugged.

'I reckon I'll give it away, but I don't yet know how.'

He nodded at Hardy.

'Untie him and set him free too.'

Strongbow assented.

The Growl didn't wait any longer. He stepped out of the wreckage of the shack and found his horse, who was pawing the ground impatiently. Mounting with remarkable swiftness, the strange doglike rider jerked the reins and went off without looking back. He had saved the United States of America from an outrageous plot but he wanted no congratulations. The shaman in the cave had taught him how to live without reward.

He would have ridden off into the sunset, as traditional heroes do, but he was already at the western limit of the continental landmass. He had no desire to ride into the ocean. So he went south.

And as he went, he howled and growled.

Chapter Two
Jalamity Kane

She rode to the crest of the hillock and looked down. The other rider was a pale shadow on the trail below and in the moonlight his shadow was even paler than he was. That was because of the mica in the rocks which gleamed, glittered and shone and turned the landscape into something ethereal and strange. With a low snarl, she spurred her horse forwards.

She zigzagged down the slope and still the other rider didn't hear her. Was he engrossed in his private thoughts? That must be the answer. Her Winchester was cradled in her arms and her low snarl turned into a stealthy laugh. Her prey seemed oddly incautious, but this was to her advantage. At the base of the slope she spurred her mount to a fast canter.

The other rider finally became aware that something was behind him. As he turned in his saddle, she raised the rifle and aimed at his face. She slowed in order to be sure of hitting him square.

'Hey, what's this?' he cried in astonishment.

His head, which was that of a giant rabbit,

bobbed up and down, his nose twitched and his long ears undulated.

'Howdy, pard,' she said, and then she added, 'I guess you think I'm just a bandit, some unwashed desperado who wants your money. But that's not true at all. My name is Jalamity Kane and I'm hunting all the men who are part animal. I know what it means that you're a man-rabbit, it means that you studied with a shaman, one of the Mojave wizards.'

'Well, yes I did,' answered the other rider.

'I make the same speech every time I find one of you people. When I was younger and full of hope and desire, I also sought out a shaman to study with. I found one. Seven years in a subterranean cavern, putting myself through horrid exercises, expanding my mind! But it didn't work, I didn't acquire the power. I failed and my soul became bitter. It's not nice to be *bitter* and that's especially true when I look upon your *sweet* little visage. Gonna blow a hole right through it. Say your final prayers, bunny boy!'

The other rider raised a paw to remonstrate with her but it was too late. Her finger squeezed the trigger and the canyon echoed with the shot. He slumped in the saddle and his horse bolted. He didn't fall off but remained in place, his feet held by the stirrups. Jalamity watched him vanish into the crystalline darkness. She said to herself, 'I'll destroy all of you. I have no interest in money. I have no interest in anything, only in slaying every cat-man, owl-man, worm-man and cougar-man in the land. You'll see!'

It was her mission in life. A cruel and futile mission, but a mission all the same, and a gal's gotta have a mission.

When The Growl left Punta Arena, he decided not to retrace his journey back to the place he had been when he first saw Danny Bangs robbing a bank. That had been a town called Wickenburg in Arizona and he had been there thanks to a rumour he had been following up.

The rumour concerned the killers of his former boss. You see, when he was still Bill Bones, before he ever imagined he would become The Growl, his boss on that newspaper in St Louis had been something of a friend as well as a man who sent him on assignments. Ridley Smart was his name, a hardworking fella but polite nonetheless, a gentleman.

Bill had been sent to investigate the shaman in the cave and while trapped by the rockfall in the middle of nowhere, Ridley was murdered in a brawl in an uptown restaurant for no good reason. In fact, he wasn't shot full of holes even for a *bad* reason. No reason at all. The Growl learned about this much later, his transformation complete, and he decided to avenge his boss. He would find the assassins of Ridley and punish them.

But it had proved difficult to locate the bunch.

He wasn't sure how many of them there were. Some sources said six, others said seven, eight, even nine. It would take a lot of snooping before he really could be sure. And luck was an important factor too. So when he heard whisperings that a stranger who liked to hurt random people in restaurants was hanging around Wickenburg, he wasted no time riding there to see for himself.

Turned out the rumour was a false clue. But anyway, that's where he'd met Danny Bangs and that meeting had led to him saving the White House and the government from destruction. Long story, already told. But when he left Punta Arena, he saw no point returning to Arizona. Any direction was as good as any other, and he decided to ride due south.

He preferred to avoid the bigger cities when he could help it, on account of his appearance, but he had a hankering to see San Francisco anyway. He'd never been there and it was said to be a pleasant and cultured city. He might even stop off at Santa Rosa on the way, catch a play in a theatre maybe, or opera in one of the new opera houses. Get himself some culture. The Growl missed St Louis in many ways, the music and sophistication.

Also the chance to have a hot bath. Although, as he was part dog, a muddy pool was usually enough to satisfy his craving for regular ablutions, the human part of him sometimes dreamed of steamy water and soap bubbles, a scrubbing brush with soft bristles, and clean towels.

He had no intention of going back to St Louis. Someone might recognise him there, despite the radical change in his looks, and it would be quite painful for him to wander his old haunts while feeling excluded from them thanks to the severe modification of his circumstances.

So it would be San Francisco and maybe Santa Rosa. There was a strange mood permeating all of California these days, a wild abandon. The fact he had the head of a dog wouldn't be ridiculed *as much* here as in most other states. It wasn't inconceivable that he would be admired for his canine qualities. With a grin, he slowly relaxed in his saddle.

Something ahead caught his attention. A cat! His horse just wanted to keep going in a straight line, but The Growl's instincts took over. He barked and tried to chase the furtive shape as it slipped away into the undergrowth. He threw his head back and howled. Cats always distracted him, as did balls and bones. That was something his strength of will couldn't control. He accepted it as part of his nature. He rode after the darned critter.

His dog mind was in charge now. How dare cats exist in the world? It was wrong. They ought to be chased outta town and town in their case meant all the universe. Cats shouldn't oughta be allowed to live. He barked, yapped, howled, his cowl slipping off his head as he shook himself all over with delight, rage and anticipation. The cat yowled ahead.

It was almost as if the calico varmint was guiding him through the bushes by giving away its position. The Growl didn't stop to consider whether this was the case or not. He was just delighted to be on the trail of the feline fancy-pants in his natural fur coat of white, orange and black. And so he rode due east with all thoughts of San Francisco and Santa Rosa wiped out of his mind. Cats have priority. That is the immutable rule.

Jalamity was in position to ambush her next victim. She squatted in the shallow pit she had dug. The dry plain extended all around here, as flat as a tune played on a badly-maintained piano in a rotten old saloon somewhere in the worst kind of decayed ghost town where the railroad was supposed to come but didn't. She had constructed her own cover because there was no natural cover available in the geography of the bland landscape.

The rider was a puff of dust at the limits of her vision. It was early evening and he was evidently trying to cover as many miles as possible before night fell and she chuckled at the malevolent thought that he was hurrying to his doom, a circumstance he would soon be aware of. The Winchester was firm in her grasp and she chewed a stick of liquorice root.

This wasn't European liquorice or *Glycyrrhiza glabra* which also grew in a few places in a few states, having been brought over by settlers, but the harsher *Glycyrrhiza lepidota* that the Zuni people had liked to chomp as a medicine. Not that Jalamity needed a cure for anything. She just liked to chew on something at the end of a day and she hated tobacco.

She waited patiently as the cloud of beige dust that was the rider expanded in size and took on more of a familiar shape. His horse was tiring a little and his pace was slowing. As he approached, she saw that he wore a hood. All of these fools liked to cover their telltale faces!

She stood up straight, rising out of the pit like a snake about to strike, and strike she would, by which we mean attack and not cease working because of dissatisfaction with pay. She cared nothing for wealth. No ordinary bandit, this Jalamity, half woman and half man, the product of seven years' meditation that hadn't worked out the way she'd wanted.

'Hey, what's this?' he cried in astonishment.

His head, which was that of a giant squirrel, bobbed up and down, his nose twitched and his jaws chattered.

'Howdy, pard,' she said, and then she added, 'I guess you think I'm just a bandit, some unwashed desperado who wants your money. But that's not true at all. My name is Jalamity Kane and I'm hunting all the men who are part animal. I know what it means that you're a man-squirrel, it means that you studied with a shaman, one of the Mojave wizards.'

It was the same speech, or nearly the same speech as before. It was a short speech but one she had made dozens of times. Very few people ever got to hear it more than once, apart from herself.

An occasional victim escaped her, but it was such a rare event that in terms of statistics it counted for nothing at all.

Jalamity was now reaching the end of the speech. 'Gonna blow a hole right through ya. Say goodbye, squirrel boy!'

The other rider raised a paw to remonstrate with her but it was too late. Her finger squeezed the trigger and the plains absorbed the sound of the shot. First he slumped in the saddle and then he fell off. His horse didn't bolt but remained where it was, looking confused. One day, Jalamity knew, she would meet a man who was half horse. What would the horse he rode on do then? Would it regard Jalamity as an enemy of all horses and try to kick her? She had no idea. It was a riddle that only the future could solve.

Most horses didn't care about their riders but that one might be different. It was better to wait to find out the answer for sure. Speculation was a waste of her time. She climbed out of the pit, moved to the side, leaned over and reached out with her hands and jerked her wrists.

An unseen blanket came up in her fingers. Her horse was beneath it, lying on its side, and now it got clumsily to its hooves. She had covered it with a sheet and covered the sheet with sand and gravel and grit so that it resembled only the smallest of humps in the almost featureless plain. There had been nowhere else to hide it. She could have dug a pit, as she had for herself, but that would have been very hard work. Alternatively, she could have covered herself with a sheet too, but that would have restricted her visibility. Everything had worked out for the best. The squirrel-man was dead.

And now she had his horse as well. She could maybe use his horse as some part of a trap for her next victim. Killing these beasts was her mission in life. A cruel and futile mission, as we already have been told, but yes, a mission all the same, and a gal's gotta have a mission.

The Growl continued to follow the cat through the undergrowth. Soon the mass of bushes opened out into more rocky land. The cat stayed always just ahead of its pursuer, leading The Growl onwards.

He should have suspected some funny business at this stage, but he didn't. His callow canine nature had taken over his brain completely. He was enjoying the chase for its own sake, although a large part of him wanted to catch the cat. What he would do with it if he caught it was unknown to him. He might sniff at it and then let it go. He wasn't a savage.

The cat kept glancing back over its shoulder and it seemed to be smiling a sneaky smile. Eastwards they went, the vista changing as they proceeded, and a few hours later his horse was too tired to continue. The Growl growled at this. It was unlucky but he had to allow his mount to rest. Anything else would be cruel and unfair and The Grow loved animals.

Yes, even though he was part dog, with the desire to bite deeply ingrained in him, and a visceral loathing of cats, he despised casual bloodletting and even that loathing was founded on a bedrock of amusement. In other words, he found it *amusing* to loathe cats, and so didn't really loathe them at all. It was an act, a role he liked to play on an instinctive level.

He dismounted and tethered his horse to one of the lonely trees in a blasted landscape of crumbling boulders. To his astonishment, the cat didn't run off, but stopped too, waiting. The Growl made camp and the cat made camp thirty yards away. If he stepped closer to it, it moved away. If he moved back, it moved back too. It wanted to be near him, yes, but not fall into his clutches. It was playing a game with him! That was very intriguing.

He rested under the tree and his tongue lolled out of his mouth as he slept. He dreamed a muddle of dreams and they included scenes from his former life as a newspaperman, and scenes perhaps from his future life, which were blazes of soft colour and full of abstract shapes. He heard accordion music and saw a pair of shoes dancing and it was very odd.

He awoke and mounted his refreshed stallion and the chase recommenced and the cat bounded off with a definite grin on its face. He wasn't imagining it. This feline was smiling broadly. But why?

The pursuit went on all morning and most of the early afternoon and quite a large distance was covered. Considering how small the cat's legs were, it was capable of a fair lick of speed. Now they came to a lonely train track. The tracks went off to vanishing points in both directions. The rails hummed in the breeze, a melancholy music. A dull throbbing came to his ears. The rails were vibrating. A train was coming! A steam locomotive.

He saw the puff of dense black smoke rise above the horizon and he heard the growing rumble and for a few minutes he forgot all about the cat. In fact he sat on his horse not more than a yard away from the cat, who also sat and gazed at the oncoming train. Trains are interesting, they need to be watched, waved at too sometimes, even if the passengers open the windows and throw orange peel at you or poke out their rascal tongues.

The train slowed as it neared the spot where The Growl waited. The track at this point was a little warped and the driver was aware of this. He moved at a crawl now and suddenly the cat sprang with a triumphant yowl and jumped up and scrambled through one of the open doors in the side of one of the carriages. It turned and looked back at The Growl.

'Why, you! I oughta!' cried the cowled hero in dismay.

Then he realised he wasn't helpless.

The cat hadn't really defeated him, not if he was bold and quick, and not if he was willing to leave his horse behind.

He was. He dismounted, ran after the train, grabbed the edge of the door as the locomotive increased speed, hauled himself in. His horse gazed after him in a mood of supreme indifference. The Growl laughed. The cat hastened along the length of the carriage to get away from him. He followed and the passengers he passed turned up their noses at him.

His cowl had slipped, revealing too much of his snout. He adjusted it. Now the shadows that the cowl threw over his face were replaced, and so he was safe again from the outraged scrutiny of so-called ordinary folk, those hypocrites and scoundrels, at least until it slipped again. Maybe he should consider ditching the cowl for a mask? Worth thinking about.

One of the guards approached him and demanded to see his ticket. 'Didn't get a chance to buy one,' The Growl said.

'You'd better pay at the next station,' said the guard.

'I came looking for my cat.'

He pointed at the feline, who was sitting on a vacant seat and licking a paw and the guard said,

'Well, you found it now. So just sit quietly and get off at the next station, both of you. Okay?'

'What's the next station?' asked The Growl.

'Denver, Colorado.'

'Can I just sit with my cat?'

The guard nodded briskly. This seemed a reasonable request. He had a cat of his own and he understood the need of a lap to be occupied by a sentient ball of fur. 'But don't make trouble.'

The Growl had no intention of making trouble. He moved towards the cat, picked it up, sat back down, and the cat curled up and fell asleep. He stroked it. His human nature had returned to dominate his dog nature. The cat's fur felt odd to his fingertips but he didn't worry.

Some cats have more wiry hair than others.

That's all there was to it.

He stared out of the window, still stroking the sleeping cat, and pretty soon he began to feel sleepy himself. The rocking motion of the train was soothing. It was like being a child again, he thought. Not that he could ever remember being a child. The process of transmuting into a man-dog had wiped out large portions of his memory. He couldn't recall his family except as vague looming shapes, a mother that smelled of apples, a father that smelled of sawdust, and a sister who squawked like a demented parrot. His life might have been eventful before those months in the cave or perhaps not.

Bill Bones he had once been, now he was The

Growl. As for the cat on his lap, well, a cat was a cat was a cat.

Slowly he slumped in his seat and slept.

She was in a wide valley full of yucca palms and these trees made superb cover for her and her two horses. One of these horses, the one that had belonged to the squirrel-man, was out in the open, grazing on a few weeds. It would attract and distract any traveller who came near it. And shortly after he was attracted, while he was distracted, she would pounce.

Jalamity Kane had oiled her Winchester. It was starting to misfire and she needed a new one, or maybe something even more powerful, perhaps even one of the British big-game guns she'd occasionally seen, the Purdey, for example, with a kick fierce enough to dislocate the shoulder if not gripped with firmness, but she would probably have to go out East to get her hands of such a thing. In the meantime, the Winchester would do. It would do for the very next meeting she had with any kind of man-beast.

She waited, secure in the knowledge that she was a crack shot and sharp in her senses. There was a rustling above and behind her but she ignored it. Just a bird in the tree. It was the next rider that came along the trail that interested her and she concentrated on surveying the valley before her at ground level. That a stranger might enter her reality from *above* simply never occurred to her. Every man-beast she had met so far had acted more like a man than a beast, riding on a horse the same as any cowboy would.

That's why she was wholly unprepared when a hairy weight dropped onto her shoulders and knocked her into the dust. Her reflexes were fast and with an ungainly roll and twist she was clear and on her feet again. She turned and her rifle arm came up. No time to aim. The shot went wide. It had been worth the chance. And now she blinked rapidly.

She saw what had assaulted her, a pre-emptive strike by a monkey-man, a snarling primate of outrageous size.

'Lookee! It's a goddamn monkey and –'

But the monkey was faster.

It lunged forward, gripped her arms, shook her until she dropped her rifle, and then it headbutted her in the face.

Her nose was crushed, Blood spurted everywhere. Half blinded, she turned and twisted herself free of his grip. He was strong indeed, even though he was a monkey and not an ape, some sort of capuchin rather than a gorilla, but massive, with well-developed shoulders. Jalamity was outclassed in strength, agility and speed. And she had dropped her rifle.

She fell to her knees and groped for it while the monkey-man danced in an imperfect circle around her. 'Just you wait, you cotton-pickin' varmint, I'll plug ya full of lead, you'll see!' she cried.

'Oo,' came the reply.

Some part of her response was automatic. Her conditioned reflexes were taking over. She heard herself saying, 'I guess you think I'm just a bandit, some unwashed desperado who wants your money.' She paused to wipe away blood that had trickled onto her lips. 'But that's not true at all. My name is Jalamity Kane and I'm hunting all the men who are part animal.' She coughed for a few seconds and choked a little. The pain in her broken nose was dreadful. 'I know what it means that you're a man-monkey, yeah, it means that you studied with a shaman, one of the Mojave wizards.'

'Oo,' came the reply.

'Is that all you got to say to me?'

'Oo,' came the reply.

'Reckon I deserve a better response than that.'

'Oo,' came the reply.

'When I find my rifle I'm going to turn you into a sieve, you rotten hirsute son of a hairy chump. I'm gonna –'

The monkey-man drew a banana from his holster and stabbed her arm with it, as if it was a Bowie knife. 'Hey!' she objected. He stabbed her again and this time the banana erupted into bruised peel and mangled flesh. Then he pulled out a second fruit from his other holster.

'Those aren't guns or knives,' she roared.

'Oo,' was all he said.

He stabbed her again. The banana broke open immediately and dripped its thick yellow gunk all over her hair.

He raced up the nearest yucca palm and began to swing from one branch to another, then leaping to another tree, and so on, until he was lost to sight. With a curse, Jalamity climbed unsteadily to her feet. The blood was drying around her squashed nose. The monkey-man had escaped her vengeance. It wasn't the first time a man-beast had bested her, but it was the worst humiliation of her defeats, and her brain was pounding with rage.

'Don't you know what I am?' she shouted after the retreating figure high in the trees. 'Don't you know?' Then it occurred to her that he probably didn't, not least because she liked to keep herself out of the limelight, all the better for her schemes to work. But she finished her rant anyway. It's always worthwhile finishing a rant. 'I'm Jalamity Kane!'

A new rifle? Yes, but she would also need two six-shooters from now on, and a knife, maybe even a tomahawk.

The Growl woke up with a start. He realised that a weight, slight but significant, had vacated his lap. The cat was gone.

'Heck!' He was on his feet immediately.

'Meeow,' said the cat.

It was crouched by the open door.

The train was slowing, but there was no station in sight. They were still in the wilderness. It must be because the rails were warped. Even as he watched, a further slowing allowed the cat to leap out. It landed safely on the ground. The Growl called out a warning or maybe an objection, he wasn't sure which, and at once the train picked up speed.

The cat was going to get away forever unless he moved fast. He didn't stop to think about the consequences.

He jumped and rolled over the ground.

The cat was waiting for him.

Now it scurried away.

He loped along after it, his strides long and easy, despite the pain in his left ankle where he had landed badly.

His minor injury would repair itself as he went along. His body was fast at repairing itself, another of the abilities he had developed after his six months of meditation in that cave. An injury that might take a normal man five days to get over, he could get over in four and a half, four and three-quarters tops. It didn't sound so big an improvement, but in this game every minute counted, the game of the Old West, worse than chess.

The cat led him on what would have been a wild goose chase if it wasn't a cat, but it was certainly wild, both the animal and the chase. Through canyons of increasing thinness they went, up slopes and down them, round towering pillars of rock that had been carved by the windborne sand into fantastical shapes, one or two of which resembled displaced sea monsters. The sun beat down and The Growl panted from all the strain.

What kind of cat was this? Not natural, he decided. And then they passed a cave mouth and The Growl saw something inside from the corner of his eye. He knew what was in there, he knew this was another shaman cave, that the shaman within was waiting for a new disciple. They were always waiting for disciples, a part of their mission on the Earth.

But he raced onwards, committing the location to memory but making no attempt to enter and engage the shaman in talk. The cat was more important. An hour flew by, another, a third. The cat refused to tire and this was baffling and a little unnerving too. And yet it was a cat of *some* kind and he was a dog of *some* kind, so there was no help for it. He had to keep going. The desert became less harsh, the region of boulders gave way to a gentle wooded area. They weaved in and out of the trees. Birds chirped.

Suddenly there was a clearing and a shack in the middle of the space with a smoking chimney and a wide-open door and a man standing on the threshold of that door with a long Kentucky rifle.

The cat ran up to him, vanished between his legs into the shack and that is when the man with the gun said, 'Cute little fella, ain't he? Done me proud. He always gets someone new for me.'

The Growl stopped and caught his breath.

The rifle was pointed directly at him. The man in the doorway said with a sigh, 'I don't enjoy shooting folks, but I need to fund my inventions, and this is the only way of doing that. I'm an inventor but the government rejected me and now I raise money by luring and robbing. My cat is a machine, see, powered by a combination of clockwork and chemicals. His name is Chasey, very apt, don't you think? My name is Hermit Chumps and that's all you need to know. Now I will just squeeze the trigger here.'

His finger tightened on the trigger of the Kentucky rifle and there was the telltale click, but no detonation in the barrel. Instead a length of cord connected to the trigger was pulled taut. This cord ran along the ground and through a set of hooped pegs and up a pole that was adjacent to the shack. The cord rang a bell at the top of the pole and the vibrations made an unstable cairn of small flat stones on the shack's roof topple over.

The stones fell into a bowl of water, spilling the excess liquid over the rim. The liquid was soaked up by an orange cloth that grew heavier as a result. It slid down the sloped roof, pulling a sack behind it on a chain. The Growl watched in amazement, amusement and in horror too. The entire contraption was rather an elaborate device, with pulleys and springs. The cloth dragged the sack over the edge of the roof and it struck the ground.

The sack broke open. Furious bees swarmed out and flew at a stuffed bear standing nearby that was filled with some chemical that reacted violently to bee stings. The bees attacked and the bear swelled up and exploded. The explosion activated with sound waves a membrane that set off a spring that tipped a lever into the down position. The lever pulled a string that allowed sand to pour from a bottle into a weighing scale that in turn was connected to another cord. This new cord was looped around a pulley.

The Growl was baffled.

His eyes followed the probable progress of this sequence and he saw that a crossbow concealed in the bushes would shoot a bolt directly at him in the next ten seconds. That was the climax of this chain of cause and effect. The inventor clearly loved complexity for its own sake. The Growl realised that this was his weak point. He shook his head and said:

'I reckon you are mad.'

Then he took three steps to the left, out of the line of sight of the crossbow, which now discharged its bolt into empty air. But Hermit Chumps laughed and said, 'Maybe, but *you* are simple.'

The Growl frowned at this strange accusation, and then he screamed as the jaws of the bear-trap snapped shut on his legs. Hermit Chumps cried, 'Yeah, I anticipated that victims would look around when I pulled the rifle trigger and that they would then spot the crossbow. They always move out of the way to the left when they see it, so that's where I put the metal teeth on springs. You can't outwit me, you know. I am smart!'

The crossbow bolt had missed The Growl but it had struck a target and the target fell over and pulled another cord and this cord released a chock holding a weight, which swung and pulled yet another cord. This cord drew out a peg that was the only thing preventing a spiked weight on a rope from swinging down on The Growl and killing him instantly.

Hermit Chumps was saying, 'I'm one of the best inventors in the country. I studied with Gunsmith Ghouls, I did. That noble old fella taught me all he knew and some things he didn't know.'

The peg was now almost wholly out. The Growl was finished. He scowled and clenched his fists. All because of a cat. It wasn't even a real cat but a breed of automaton. No wonder its fur had felt strange, rough and unpleasant. As The Growl prepared himself for death, he considered what regrets he had. He would have to give San Francisco a miss this time, he thought ruefully, and allow those killers of his boss to remain free.

Hermit Chumps was giggling. Then he was moaning.

A hole opened up in his face.

A shot right between his eyes! The wound appeared a fraction of an instant before the sound reverberated around the clearing. Hermit Chumps stood erect a few seconds more, tottering this way and then that. He finally fell backwards, an angry smile on his mouth, into the shadows of the shack, his feet protruding into the daylight like two filthy corncobs.

The Growl swung his head around. Jalamity Kane's next shot knocked the peg back into its hole, securing the weight and preventing it from swinging. She shouldered her Winchester and strolled casually across the clearing to the trap. She examined it, inserted her rifle like a lever and prised the jaws apart. With a gasp, The Growl limped away from it.

'Saved your life, pard,' said Jalamity, 'because I don't want anyone else to take it. That's my privilege, see?'

'Yes, I felt certain we might meet again.'

'Been killing man-beasts.'

'How ladylike of you, miss.' The Growl spoke with bitter irony. The pain in his legs made him wince. He added:

'Real cutie, ain't ya?'

'Listen up, doggy. I have killed a moose-man, a squirrel-man, a skunk-man and a rabbit-man since we last met. I really enjoyed killing that rabbit. He was a vile specimen if ever there was one.'

'You killed a rabbi?'

'Not a rabbi, a rabbit, a massive rabbit. A man-rabbit, in fact. I suppose the human part may have been a rabbi. Then he'd have been a rabbi-rabbit, but my doubts on that score are profound.'

'If he'd had rabies,' said The Growl significantly, 'he'd have been ... But I am reluctant to say it.' He shrugged.

He was obsessed with rabies and this was because of his doglike nature. It was a major concern for him, just as a concern with mousse might seem obvious and natural to a demented moose.

'A rabid rabbi-rabbit?' said Jalamity.

'Reckon,' he replied.

'Anyway,' she said, and she winked at him as she spoke the words, 'better to get the unpleasant part over with.'

She turned her Winchester on him, only to find that he wasn't there. Quick as an oiled shadow, he had limped off at a tremendous rate into the undergrowth and was already accelerating away.

'Damn you, doggy!' she snarled, as she ran after him. With injured legs, it was unlikely he would be able to maintain this pace for long. She was confident she would get him soon. She conserved her energy, making sure she never quite lost sight of him ahead. But he weaved erratically and it would have been nearly impossible to get a good shot at him.

'Why are you so eager to remain alive?' she shouted after him, but she had no hopes of receiving an answer and didn't. They ran for hours, and though she was unaware of the fact, he was retracing his steps. This was the same way he'd come when chasing the fake cat.

The daylight was fading when he came to the cave he had passed earlier. It was his true destination. His legs were burning and he was weak, but he dipped behind the cover of a big boulder.

She approached the cave and she heard noises inside it. She smiled a grim smile. She assumed he had taken refuge inside the cave. Without hesitating, she rushed straight into it. The Growl stepped out from his hiding place. He knew a lot about these shaman caves. A revolver appeared in his gloved left hand and he fired at an oblique angle into the ceiling. His aim was true, the rocks started tumbling and blocking the entrance.

Jalamity understood that the prey had turned the tables and lured her into a trap. Before the cave was fully sealed, he shouted into it, 'You will be sealed in there for months, maybe years. There's a shaman to keep you company. Maybe this time you will learn properly.'

'I already did the meditation!' she cried. 'I am already half woman, half man. I don't need to do it again.'

'A woman and a man combined? No, miss, that's just a person. *One* being. A *person*. Now you have the chance to learn how to transform into some other creature. It's what you wanted, ain't it? Why, it don't even have to be a proper animal. Can be anything you like.'

The rockfall had finished and the cave mouth presented a solid barricade of rocks. He could no longer understand what she was saying. Her words were just audible but their meaning was unclear.

He shrugged and spoke for his own benefit. 'Night's coming on and I need to rest my injured legs. Then I need to find a substitute horse. Reckon I'll be off. Should be a good camping spot not far. Won't be seeing you in the morning, so I will say my farewells now, miss.'

And he limped off into the gathering dusk.

He thought about her.

His best guess was that she would be in the cave for five years. It depended on the skills of the shaman inside.

As it happened, Jalamity remained in that cave for ten years. The Growl had long since emigrated when she freed herself. He was sitting far away on a chair on his porch, sipping tea from a gourd and gazing at the pampas. She eventually emerged as part unicorn, vowing a revenge that she would never take. The horn in the centre of her forehead was enormous. She stood in the sunlight, hands on her hips, blinking at the bright sky.

The shaman came out after her, wanting to impart one last word of wisdom to a dedicated pupil, but she turned on him with a snarl. He saw the threat in her eyes and he realised that the bond between them was broken. Forced to learn the mystical ways, she was resentful.

He turned to run, but she was quicker.

She hated all magic now, even the magic that had partly changed her into one of the most magnificent creatures ever to exist on the planet. And she was so nimble-hooved that she caught up with him after only a few steps. Her horn found its mark. She tossed her head.

Up flew the shaman, neatly impaled in the vital place that can't be talked about in polite society. He was flung over some bushes. As he flew, he grasped his buttocks in both hands and wept.

Two lawmen happened to be passing on the other side of the bushes. They saw a flying man and supposed he was levitating through the power of his mind alone, a sight worthy of much respect.

But as he narrowly missed them in his descent while screaming a series of unspiritual oaths, their admiration for his telekinetic abilities rapidly declined and they revised their opinion of him.

He was clearly just another impolite rogue who happened to be airborne, a vulgar specimen. The one called Crock squinted and said, 'No sweat,' and his companion, who was called Brawls, adjusted his hat and answered, 'Actually it's a bit sweaty.' And so they rode on.

Chapter Three
Chain of Command

He was riding south, heading Mexico way, and following the coast, and during the night of the full moon the ocean glittered to his right, But he kept the cowl over his head and only a few wisps of white hair fell across his forehead, even milkier in the moonlight. An old man?

No there was too much vitality in his form, stooped as it was, for he didn't ride straight in the saddle but was hunched forward, and there was a grim smile on his lips, and he held the reins loosely, the white gloves on his hands gleaming like monstrous teeth as he cantered.

A shot rang out, grazing his shoulder, and he slowed his pace. Maybe an ordinary fella would have spurred his mount even faster into a gallop, but not this rider, not The Growl. He turned to peer at the source of the shot. Something was moving on the surface of the sea.

A hand was thrust out of the water and it was holding a revolver. Now the bubbles rose around it and burst and the rest of the diver slowly emerged. Was he a deep-sea explorer who had got lost on the murky seabed? The Growl waited for the armoured suit to be fully exposed.

The diver shouted and his words were muffled in his helmet. 'Hands up! I won't hesitate to fill you full of lead.'

'Easy, pard,' said The Growl, who'd caught the gist of his meaning. With fluid grace he lifted both arms high. 'Waterproof Colt, huh? Amazing the things they come out with. Always a surprise.'

'Yeah, he's waterproof,' mumbled the diver, as he approached the shore. It was a strange misunderstanding. The Growl saw that his assailant was mounted on a young male horse that was also encased in a pressurised suit. The sight was so unexpected that he burst into laughter.

'No laughing matter,' bellowed the diver. 'I'm a robber, see? And I got the most original hold-up method in the West. I hide offshore and nobody suspects I am in the deep blue waiting for 'em.'

The Growl knew that the armour would probably deflect a bullet, but there was a weak spot on the suit, the valve on the crown of the helmet where the suit connected with the hose that provided air. The Growl's arms were raised straight up. Suddenly there was a gun in his left hand. He squeezed the trigger and sent a bullet directly up. It was like he was firing into the air in celebration. The diver was too bewildered to take any action.

'Huh? What was the point of that, pard?' he cried.

'Plunging fire,' said The Growl.

What goes up must come down, a difficult shot but not an impossible one, and the bullet whistled a steep descent and punctured the rubber hose at a point near the valve. The diver struggled to remove his helmet. He knew something was wrong but he wasn't sure what.

The Growl straightened his left arm and fired again.

The diver's gun flew out of his grasp. His horse panicked and churned the water into bright froth. 'Whoa there!'

'Dunno where your pump is, but one thing's for sure. You won't be doing any more hold-ups tonight,' said The Growl, and then he added as he spurred his own horse onward, 'If you try it, you'll drown. Now I don't know who you are but I'm too busy for such games.'

He rode on, thoughtful. He was heading Mexico way because he'd picked up a clue that one of the killers of his former boss was hiding down in Baja, not far from the town of Loreto, and he wanted to check it out. He was a patient man but the desire for vengeance inside him never cooled. The eccentric diver with his original robbery method was a distraction, nothing more, at least that's how he reasoned at the present moment.

Later, the incident would give him an idea that proved useful. He pressed on and reckoned he would be in San Diego before morning. He would rest for a while, more for the sake of his horse than himself. Then he would cross over the border and keep going. It would be tough riding the barren wastelands of Baja's interior, but he was hardened to deprivations and in fact he almost welcomed the coming ordeal. Grimly, he smiled.

The beating of wings came out of the dark sky. Something swooped and he twisted his head to avoid a pair of vicious talons. Again, the gun was in his left hand with the slickness of a thought.

'Go for his eyes, Horus!' came a shout.

The hawk, or whatever it was, swooped again, and a sharp talon caught in the fabric of the cowl and pulled it off. The raptor screamed in triumph, soared up and dropped its prize before folding its wings to dive again. The Growl took immediate evasive action, jerking his horse first one way, then another, all the time edging closer to where the voice had come from. He kept his gun trained on the elusive dark shape in the sky.

The moonlight gleamed on the tail feathers for an instant and The Growl could have blasted the bird into avian heaven, but abruptly he turned and fired into the night instead. There was a yowl and The Growl spurred his horse in the direction of the sound. The hawk missed him again and rose high, waiting for further instructions that never came.

The Growl found his assailant rubbing a bruised head. His bullet had hit the boulder the man was sheltering under and knocked off a chunk of rock that fell into his skull. His cranium was bruised but no permanent damage had been done and now the fella looked up in fright.

'I daresay you won't set that bird on me again.'
'Horus? He's my pet.'

'You use him as part of your hold-up act?'

The robber shrugged.

'You must admit it's original,' he replied.

'Yeah, I do, but not quite as original as one I went through earlier. I never knew this stretch of coastline was so packed with villains.' His voice was a low rasp and, lacking the cowl, his head was a fearsome thing to behold. The robber began trembling and The Growl laughed.

'I dunno who you are and I ain't too interested. I got things to do that are no concern of yours,' he muttered.

And he rode off, leaning in the saddle to retrieve his cowl as he did so, an impressive piece of horsemanship. South he kept going and he topped a rise and the lights of San Diego twinkled in the distance. He nodded in satisfaction and a moment's distraction was all it took.

The flute music came from the dunes to his left. It was haunting, disturbing yet serene, exotic and unusual. It made The Growl feel instantly sleepy. That in itself was alarming enough, but his keen ears picked up the telltale slither of a deadly menace. He shook his head roughly to clear the mental cobwebs from his brain and then he pulled on the reins.

His horse pranced forwards and to the side. The snake had launched itself into the air and missed his face by inches. What kind of snake could move *that* fast? It wasn't a local species. It was big, much bigger than a rattler, which was the only kind of venomous snake you got in southern California. This was the most astoundingly agile snake he'd ever seen. The flute controlled it, the same way a puppet master pulls the strings.

But the strings were notes and little snatches of tune. The snake twisted its huge body and came back for him. It slid along the ground just as fast as a horse could gallop and its wedge of a head was very menacing. He jerked the reins again and managed to dodge it, but only just. Momentum carried it several feet into the dunes but it turned quickly.

The flute sounded again and directed the serpent's movements and with a sigh of exasperation, The Growl raised his left hand. The gun was in his grip in a flash and he fired into the darkness.

The flute music went off-key and was soon followed by a discordant series of low moans and then a shrill curse. The Growl noted that the snake had ceased to approach and was apparently waiting for further instructions. The cursing in the darkness continued and The Growl rode to where the unlucky robber was on his knees, his face contorted oddly.

'I aimed for your flute, pard,' said The Growl.

'And that's where you got me,' gasped the hold-up man, rocking away his pain. But he managed a sardonic smile. 'You must admit my method is original and unique to myself. A mamba!'

'Never seen one of those snakes before.'

'It's from Africa. I bought it from a zoo a few months ago. Trained it with a flute I made myself. Clever, huh?'

'I saw some stuff no less brilliant already tonight. There were six bullets in my chamber but I only have a couple left.'

'What are you gonna do with me?' he wailed.

'Don't care to reload before I have to, so I reckon I'll leave you as you are. I got business to attend to, pard.'

With an ironic wave, The Growl rode off and this time reached the outskirts of San Diego without further incident. He found an inexpensive but clean hotel, put his horse in a stable out back. He had a meal sent up to his room, preferring to eat alone than visit the dining space. Too many strange looks would be hurled his way if he showed himself in public. The fare was simple but wholesome and he drank half a bottle of good wine.

The next morning he rose early and continued his journey. He considered what had happened to him the night before. Attacked three times in less than an hour by three very strange hold-up men. He wondered why he should have been targeted by such eccentric methods.

There must be a reason for it. He decided the universe was trying to tell him something. As he went to fetch his horse from the stable, a man loomed out of the interior with a crooked smile.

'Don't I know you?'

'Can't say I've had the pleasure,' said The Growl and went to push past the man, but his way was blocked.

The voice was menacing now. 'Sure you can.'

'Nope,' said The Growl.

The glint of a long knife turned this conversation into a confrontation faster than a desperado can sink a glass of redeye. The man was covered in scars, his jaw was lopsided, the bones of his visage had been distorted by some enormous pressure. The Growl felt some empathy for him. The world wasn't an easy place for people who looked so different.

'Yet you're wearing a cowl. Reckon you are working for Monk Lewis. Am I right about that?' the man snarled.

'Pard,' said The Growl slowly, hoping to talk his way out of it but guessing that violence would be the end result, 'I ain't never heard of such a fella and the reason I wear this cowl is personal.'

The knife wove a pattern of steel inches from The Growl's face. 'Liar! The cowl is the same colour. You are one of The Chanters! You did this to my face and left me for dead. But I didn't die! Eight days crawling through the desert on my hands and knees. And now I –'

Intending to catch The Growl by surprise, the man lunged with the knife, a very supple movement, the thrust of a man who knew a lot about fighting with blades. His speed was good, his balance also, but The Growl was even faster. He snatched the knife with his left hand.

'You fool,' roared the would-be killer, 'this knife is sharp enough to cut your hand clean through.

Watch this!'

But before he could jerk the handle, the knife vanished. The man stared at the gloved hand that was now empty.

'Where the hell did it go?' he cried in amazement.

'I have it,' said The Growl.

'Conjuring trick, huh?' grumbled the man.

'Sort of. But don't go expecting me to explain my secrets to you. That'll be the day I forget to be cautious.'

The Growl waved the gloved hand and the knife was back, but now he held it and the advantage was wholly his.

'Go ahead and cut my throat. I know Monk Lewis wants me dead. Do the job your boss has told you to do.'

The Growl threw the knife and it buried itself deep into one of the wooden posts holding up the roof of the stable. He shook his head and said, 'I don't cut throats unless I really must. Don't care to cut yours none. I ain't heard of Monk Lewis or The Chanters. Got my own concerns. Figure I'll collect my horse and be on my way. Good day to you.'

The knife fighter gaped at him in disbelief.

'You can't do that!'

The Growl was already walking away. He looked over his shoulder. 'Why not? Seems to me I'm doing it.'

'But I tried to knife you! You oughta –'

'Sonny, I didn't oughta do nothin' I don't wanna. Get it? But seeing you have been polite, I can tell you a small part of my business. My boss ended up dead thanks to some ruffians. Ridley Smart was his name, good fella, and now I am seeking his killers. Heard a rumour and am investigating it. So you can see we are in a similar situation.'

The man gasped at this and said, 'Where's this rumour taking you?' and his eyes were so wide with wonder that The Growl decided to humour him a little more and so he answered gently:

'Loreto in Baja.'

The man whistled low. He approached The Growl with his hand extended for a shake. 'That's where I'm headed too. I also heard a rumour. Seems that The Chanters are down that way.'

The Growl declined to shake the hand. It would have alarmed the man too much to feel paws behind the fabric of those gloves. The man looked dismayed at the refusal, but then shrugged it off. He said, 'Maybe Monk Lewis is there, I reckon it's highly probable.'

'I ride alone,' said The Growl.

'Heck, how did you know I was going to suggest I come with you? But it makes good sense. Two men in that desert stand a better chance than one. Plus when we reach Loreto … Well, you'll get the men you're hunting for, and I'll get the ones I'm after. No sweat.'

The Growl studied the man more carefully, looking him up and down, and on an impulse he said, 'Fine.'

'Fine? Meaning I can go with you?'

'Sure. Why not?'

'Is that a proper question? The answer is because you ride alone, you said. Why did you have a change of heart? But I guess it was one of those rhetorical questions, not to be answered?'

'Something about you,' said The Growl.

'What kind of thing?'

'I had a change of heart because you seem to be a man who's all *heart*. Get it now? My name is The Growl. I wear this cowl because I don't like folks who get too interested in the features of my face. That's all you need to know about me. Actually there's one other fact you should know. I like cats. I don't exactly mean that I like them to stroke.'

'You just like 'em, huh? I'm the same way about showgirls. I don't like to stroke them. Folks say I'm odd. I prefer to play games with them, not the kinds of games most men play. Chess.'

'Many men like to play that,' said The Growl.

'Not with showgirls.'

The Growl accepted this and smiled.

The man said, 'Forgot to introduce myself. Name's Jorge Luis. I was born down south, much more south than Mexico. I'll tell you all about it when we're on the trail. I'll get my horse.'

The Growl considered this change in his circumstances. For the first time since he had partly transformed into a dog, he had a travelling companion. The prospect slightly worried him. It was something he'd vowed to avoid. But Jorge seemed a decent sort. If anything went wrong, they could part company quickly enough. Nothing to panic about.

The universe was definitely trying to tell him something. Riding south into Mexico, attacked three times in quick succession by three very strange hold-up men. And now this coincidence, a man seeking vengeance on fellas who wore cowls. But what could it mean?

They crossed into Mexico without any trouble. Jorge spoke fluent Spanish and could probably talk their way out of any difficulties anyway. He was friendly, a true gentleman, he had charisma. The Growl was taciturn all the way, but this wasn't a problem. They rode hard.

Jorge did most of the talking, but even so he didn't say too much. He told how he had been born in Buenos Aires and came up north to work when one of his uncles had invited him. A long voyage by ship, docking finally at the port of Corpus Christi in Texas. Then by horse to California, where he'd made a good salary in his uncle's business, but one night he'd fallen into the clutches of The Chanters and that evil Monk Lewis.

The Growl listened but didn't respond with anything stronger than a grunt and half his mind was concentrated on his own dreams of revenge. It did occur to him that killing the killers of his boss wouldn't help Ridley Smart none, but it wasn't really about helping anyone.

It was about satisfying an inner urge that seared his soul, charring it at the edges, so that if he ever became a ghost he was convinced he would be a crisp and browned example of the type.

After two days, they approached a cave in an isolated rock formation. The mouth was narrow but the cave behind was large. The Growl said, 'I use caves to meditate in. That's what I do. I'm going in there for twenty-four hours and I don't want to be disturbed. If you don't like that and don't want to hang around then I suggest we part right now.'

'I'll wait,' responded Jorge with a nod.

The Growl entered the cave.

He was half-shaman himself now, as well as half-man and half-dog, and if those fractions don't appear to add up properly, that's because magic isn't like science and the sums come out differently. It could be stated without error that he was one-and-a-half times a creature. He sat in the place a shaman would be most likely to sit, near the back.

His mind settled into the pulse of the meditation rhythm. His focus shrank but became tighter as a result. He breathed in the required manner. The universe was trying to tell him something and now he was going to find out what exactly its message was. The answer would come if he was patient enough, and soon he was in a state of pseudo-oblivion and his consciousness was roaming the higher dimensions of the psychic substrata.

The encounters with the hold-up men had been so odd that they felt almost *magical*. It now occurred to him that magic was surely going to be a part of the adventure ahead. He must take whatever protective measures he could. It was imperative that he accurately recall the lessons of the shaman he had studied with after that fortuitous rockfall.

Time became meaningless. Hours passed but he was unaware of them and during his meditation he tuned his mind so that he would become extra sensitive to the supernatural. From now on he would be warned by a weird tingling in his spine if he was near paranormal forces. This tingling would give him a tiny but crucial advantage over normal men.

He emerged from the cave and exactly one day had passed. Jorge was still there, having made camp half a mile from the cave mouth. He was sitting on an uncomfortable rock and singing to himself. He was the sort of fella who'd play a guitar anywhere if he had a guitar.

He looked up as The Growl approached.

'Finished?' he asked.

'Yep. I learned something. Magic is real.'

'You didn't know?'

'Sure, I knew that, but what I learned is that magic is going to be a part of what we encounter on this exploit.'

'I could have told you that,' smiled Jorge.

'The Chanters, huh?'

'The powers they have are occult and Monk Lewis is a genuine sorcerer. I would be running away from him if I had any sense, but he did this to my face and I want to make him pay for it.'

The Growl nodded. He said nothing about how his lengthy mediation had given him a superior power to detect occult forces, to know when an unnatural power was being applied *before* its effects were felt directly. An early warning alarm. A normal man might have a spell thrown at him and would be unaware until the black magic struck him.

The Growl would be aware the moment the caster of the spell decided to cast it, buying him valuable time. Spells took time to cast, not just seconds but minutes. That was very useful. The price for this heightened sensitivity was that a little of his strength was sapped.

Jorge didn't need to be told any of this.

Better to keep some secrets wholly to himself, The Growl decided, though Jorge was the sort of fella one *knows* is trustworthy. The problem is that in this world even the best people can stab you in the back accidentally. The less they know, the better. That's the way it is.

Dead men tell no tales, sure enough, but deaf men don't get to know tales in the first place and that's safer.

And the best way to turn a man with good hearing deaf is never to tell him too much. The Growl's lips were sealed, and they weren't even delicate lips of fleshy pink, like most human lips.

They were black, a thin line that rimmed his teeth like lacquer. He pursed them and said, 'The rumours might be false. You realise that, don't you?

I am chasing a killer who might not be in Loreto after all. The same applies for you. This journey could be wasted, pard.'

Jorge nodded. 'It's a chance worth taking.'

'You're right. Let's go.'

The rumours were right. The man hunted by The Growl was named Traven and he was one of the bunch who had killed his former boss while he was having his dinner. It was still a riddle why Ridley Smart had been murdered in such a smart restaurant in uptown St Louis.

The Growl planned to unravel that riddle and do away with Traven. As for Jorge, his own enemies were there too, The Chanters, and they believed they'd found a perfect sanctuary and base for their nefarious activities in this pleasant but obscure town in Baja. Monk Lewis had told them that. He said they would be safe from interference down here.

Loreto is obscure in global terms but it's also one of the oldest settlements the Spanish established in the peninsula, founded in 1697 by Jesuit priests, but it had been a home for the Monqui people and sometimes the Cochimí tribes. It has a pleasant setting on the Gulf. The architecture is interesting. The climate is reasonable. All the facilities that rough desert travellers such as The Growl and Jorge might crave can be found there.

The Growl didn't ask *why* Monk Lewis and The

Chanters had tried to kill Jorge. It wasn't his business. He didn't need to know the whys and wherefores in order to act. If he came up against a villain, all that mattered was who might be quicker on the draw, and it was always him. But he wasn't overconfident. It could be the case that there were faster gunslingers around than him, though he hadn't met any yet. He'd heard vague stories about a fella called Monkey Man who was said to be the quickest of all.

Maybe The Growl would meet him one day.

Who could say for sure?

It occurred to The Growl that if they found The Chanters before they found Traven, he could compel The Chanters to tell him where Traven was hiding out and this would save a lot of time.

The Chanters, at gunpoint, could be encouraged to use their occult powers to pinpoint Traven's exact location. Because of his increased sensitivity to the presence of supernatural activity, The Growl would know if they were bluffing or genuinely using their magic to find Traven. He decided this was definitely a viable course of action. He said:

'We'll go and get your lot first, pard.'

'Really?' asked Jorge.

'Yeah, I'll help you with The Chanters and then I'll go and find my man to finish off our Mexican vacation.'

'That's very generous of you, señor.'

The Growl shrugged.

It wasn't generosity but practicality that drove

him to make that particular decision, yet he *was* a generous man at times, so he didn't dispute the definition and he felt a growing affection for his companion. This lost soul who had come all the way from Argentina by ship, and then rode west alone on a horse, just to have his face mutilated by occultists.

As they were passing a cactus, it suddenly uprooted itself and turned with a gun in a hand that poked from its body. The Growl had long experience with the oddest hold-ups and he whirled and his own revolver was in his left hand. Jorge was too stupefied to do anything.

'Drop your gun, stranger, or your pal will buy it.'

The cactus had a human voice.

Jorge was confused. 'Buy it? What is there to buy out here? I see no retail outlets of any description.'

The Growl explained, 'It means that if I don't drop my gun it will shoot you and probably kill you.'

'That's exactly what I mean,' declared the cactus. A button popped on its main trunk and now The Growl realised it wasn't a real talking plant but a man in a rubber suit. It must have been awfully hot inside there with the blazing sun and the bandit was probably desperate.

But a dehydrated man is slow to think and react.

Another button popped. The barrel poking out of the cactus wavered for an instant and then The Growl asked:

'What do you want?'

'Your valuables, amigo. Money, jewels, your guns, your horses. I want the things you can provide, all of them.'

'The bullets in the guns too?' asked The Growl.

'Of course! What kind of an idiot would I be if I didn't take the bullets as well as the guns? Hand 'em over!'

'Here's the first one,' shouted The Growl.

And he fired at the cactus.

The shot punctured the suit, passed through the man within, allowed blood to trickle out of the hole like juice, but the slug didn't emerge on the other side. The revolver wasn't powerful enough for that. The cactus started to wobble a little, then the wobbling accelerated. Soon it was rocking back and forth faster and faster while its occupant groaned.

'I reckon one was enough,' said The Growl to Jorge. 'He doesn't seem to want any of the others. Too bad.'

'That was a very accurate shot, señor.'

'Thanks. But I think I might throw this gun away and buy a more powerful model when I get the chance.'

They watched the cactus finally topple over.

It had acted drunk, as if it had swallowed too much tequila, which funnily enough is a spirit made from cactus. The bandit inside the costume was a spirit now, if spirits exist, a desert ghost.

'Let's get going,' muttered The Growl.

Jorge nodded. This ride was untypical, the cactus incident was untypical too. But untypical things were more common than typical ones in the life of The Growl and Jorge already realised this.

He had picked a very intriguing man for a travelling companion. Jorge still believed The Growl was a man, though he did begin to have doubts before they reached Loreto. When they stopped to camp or just enjoy a rest, the major clue was the way he cocked his leg when emptying his bladder against a cactus. Not quite the way a man would do it.

After many minor adventures on the route, none of which are worth telling, the pair of weary riders entered the outskirts of Loreto. Jorge asked if they ought to look for a hotel first and The Growl agreed. It was essential they get some rest before embarking on the revenge spree.

'How will we go about locating The Chanters?' Jorge wanted to know as they rode down a narrow street.

'I have my method,' said The Growl.

'Me too,' said Jorge.

The Growl turned his head to stare at him. 'Yeah? What method is that? Going into saloons and asking the landlord if he's seen them? I doubt that's the best way of doing it, pard.'

'I wasn't thinkin' that,' said Jorge.

'How will you find them then? It ain't a big town but they could be holed up anywhere in it. They might spot you before you spot them, if you get what I mean, and do worse to you than what they done last time. They know who you are, see, and that's not safe for you.'

'My method,' said Jorge with dignity, 'is to look for individuals who wear cowls on their heads. The Chanters wear cowls. Ordinary men don't. You do, I concede that point, but you're an exception. I will look for cowled men and they are the ones I shall try to kill.'

The Growl digested this. 'It's a fairly good method, I reckon. But I bet my method is better. Leave it to me.'

Jorge nodded. He fully trusted The Growl.

They kept riding slowly.

It was sunset and the streets were quiet. They found a small hotel down a narrow street and tied their horses to the hitching post. They walked inside and paid for a room with two beds.

'Good to get off the streets where you might be recognised,' The Growl said to Jorge as they climbed the staircase to the room. Jorge nodded. But was the same true for The Growl?

'Not really,' came the reply, 'because the man I am looking for, Traven, doesn't know who the hell I am. He's never seen me and he doesn't even know I am on his trail. This quest is a lot easier for me than it is for you, pard. Your desire for vengeance is personal.'

'And yours isn't?'

'Not really, not to the same degree. I liked Ridley Smart but he was only a friend, he wasn't my actual *face.'*

Jorge grinned horribly beneath his scars.

'I understand, amigo.'

'It's semi-personal, I suppose, but that's not in the same league. Yours is a true vengeance born of hatred.'

'No need to say more, señor. What shall we do for the rest of the evening? Play cards maybe? Some poker?'

'I don't play cards,' answered The Growl.

'What then? Sing songs? No? Well then, can you make duck sounds with your mouth? That's good fun.'

The Growl shook his head firmly.

'Let's get some shuteye now and in the morning we'll find The Chanters and rid the world of them. Then I'll go after Traven and rid the world of him too. It's gonna be a cleaner life.'

Jorge said, 'If we are successful against The Chanters, why don't I assist you with Traven?' But he already knew The Growl would refuse the offer. Two against a bunch is acceptable, but two against one is against the code of honour that The Growl lived by. Though it might be considered foolish to have such a chivalrous attitude in such a dangerous environment, The Growl got away with it because of the special powers he had.

'That's mighty kind of you, pard, but it ain't necessary. So get some sleep and rest that torn up visage of yours and in the morning we'll both be fresh and ready to engage in mortal combat.'

Jorge laid his head down on the pillow.

Ten minutes later he was snoring. The Growl lay on his back and studied a network of cracks on the ceiling in the dimness of the balmy night. He thought about Ridley Smart and what he knew about him. Maybe those fellas had killed him for a good reason, a reason unknown to The Growl? He assumed the attack was unprovoked and random, but what if that wasn't true? Suppose Ridley had deserved death? He'd kept his spare time activities secret from The Growl and some of those activities could have been nefarious. It was possible. But what is the point of speculating on all that?

Traven was doomed.

The Growl slipped off into sleep and his dreams were full of the full moon and the music it made inside his soul. And across the face of that moon moved shapes that were catlike, ratlike, batlike.

He blinked, opened his eyes wide, and sat up in bed. Jorge was already up and about and coming carefully up the stairs with a tray. Two steaming mugs of coffee stood on the tray. He must have fetched it from the kitchen out back. The Growl welcomed the beverage.

He said between sips, 'What time is it?'

'Six thirty. Streets are mostly quiet outside. Will be good to be out of here by seven. Then we should wander around, very warily, looking for men who are wearing cowls. Whaddya say?'

'I have a better way of finding them. Don't ask what it is. But yes, we can wander around, that's part of it. But we won't need to look for men in cowls. I will tell you when we are close.'

Jorge accepted this and drank his own coffee.

The Growl hoped to use his heightened sensitivity to supernatural events to find The Chanters while they were engaged in an occult ritual. They would be concentrating so hard on the spell or the conjuration or whatever it was they did that they might be caught off guard.

Then he would destroy most of them but keep one back and use him and his powers to locate Traven. One type of magic, his own, would be employed in order to enable him to take advantage of another type, The Chanters', and that's how missions are accomplished.

He finished his coffee and they went down the stairs together and out into the new day. They strolled at random through the mazy streets down to the sea and back again. It was a peaceful town. Nothing seemed strange or amiss. The mountains as a backdrop made an impressive sight and the blue of the Gulf was soothing to the mind. They turned and began up a street that was darker than it ought to be. It was in shadow, yes, but the shade of the buildings shouldn't have been so turgid at this time of day.

The Growl stopped.

'Wait, don't move. I'm picking up something.'

Jorge gazed at the ground.

'I don't see anything there. What are you picking up? Did someone lose a silver dollar or something?'

'A vibration, an occult resonance, that's what.'

He lifted a finger to his lips.

Jorge obeyed this instruction and remained silent. The Growl sniffed for a few moments, turned his head at an inquisitive angle. He was feeling the pulse of occult activity. He felt sure that a diabolical ritual was taking place right now in the vicinity of where they were standing. One of the houses in this street! But which? He moved forward a few steps and the sensation weakened. He stepped back and moved a foot to the side.

Yes, that was better, the sensation was gaining in strength. He took another pace to the side until he was adjacent to an old wooden door. The activity he'd detected was behind this barrier.

No doubt about it, The Chanters were in this house. And they were right in the middle of one of these obscene ceremonies. The Growl pictured the scene to himself, even though he hadn't seen The Chanters yet: the cowled figures and a presiding magician, who would be Monk Lewis, all arranged in a circle with an arcane symbol chalked on the floor.

He pressed his ear to the door and heard faint and low music. It was some song of hell or limbo, a song to warm the hearts of already overheated devils. It was a chant and chanting is what chanters do. How could he be mistaken about this? The Chanters were inside! He turned to Jorge and said, 'Our search is over and now the resolution begins.'

Jorge reached out to try the handle of the door.

To his surprise, it turned.

The door swung open. How careless of The Chanters! They probably felt so secure, considering their power, that little things such as locking doors never occurred to them. Well, too bad.

The Growl grinned.

'After you, pard,' he said.

Jorge bowed. 'No, after you, señor. I insist.'

The Growl chuckled and he rushed inside. He entered a bare room, dusty, unused for years. The music came from below, from a cellar. There were steps down and he hurried down them.

Jorge was right behind him, his gun in one hand, his knife in the other, a scowl of pure hatred on his face.

They reached the bottom step and stopped dead in their tracks. Blinking and gasping, they beheld a scene straight from the antechambers of damnation and for long moments they were overwhelmed. This was worse than anything The Growl had been anticipating.

The Chanters had been making so much noise they hadn't heard anybody enter the house or come down the cellar steps. Also they were concentrating on the ritual with such intensity there was no space in their minds left for thoughts of anything else. The focus was acute.

They were arranged in a circle, as The Growl had visualised, but the circle was an oval, elongated so that it resembled the erotic portal of a lady, and Monk Lewis was standing where the pleasure button of a lady would be. These things are awkward to discuss, but I'm sure you know what is meant. Sometimes there are subjects we must face boldly but that doesn't give us permission to be blunt and crude in our language, does it?

The Growl had extra sensitivity to occult vibrations and thus knew it was Monk Lewis but he surely would have guessed the truth anyway. For one thing, the fella was dressed differently. He wore no cowl but a tonsure. He was short, rather portly, a jolly little fellow in appearance, but that was an illusion. Among the worst of all world sorcerers, he had trained himself to summon up demonic forces through willpower and ritual.

Each individual Chanter wore a cowl, as has been stated, but the remainder of them was pure nudity. Every man in the ellipse was naked. Only Monk Lewis wore clothes, the robes of an abbot, and for some reason he still appeared more obscene than his depraved acolytes.

The Chanters sang and as they did so, the man-parts of their groins took up the rhythm and swung in time to the eldritch melodies. But these melodies were contrapuntal, in other words there were many melodies present, all different, but working together to create harmony.

This harmony wasn't discordant but it was dark, disturbing, panic-inducing and infernal all the same. The Growl didn't know much about Classical music but when he had been plain Bill Bones back in St Louis he had attended, in the company of Ridley Smart, a few concerts of music by various composers, some of which he had genuinely enjoyed.

Off the top of his head, he would say that what he was hearing now was an amalgam of twisted Offenbach with demented Gounod with rabid Donizetti and frothing Berlioz, all carved up with a scimitar and rearranged back to front. The counterpoint aspect was reminiscent of Gesualdo, that insane composer of weird madrigals who was so wildly chromatic that his singers frequently had nervous breakdowns and then breakdowns of their breakdowns, which meant they ended up being fixed and could keep singing, even though they often didn't care to by that stage. The Growl was amazed.

And the masculine pendulums of The Chanters swung menacingly as the music pushed forward through time like a speeded-up glacier, chilly, lethal, a merciless force of nature, or in this case supernature. Jorge trembled, his knees knocking together and keeping time.

Yes, his knees matched the beat of the chanted songs.

The weird ambience was ghastly.

It slowed down the reactions not only of Jorge but even of The Growl. He felt he was wading through a swamp.

And the sucking liquids of that swamp were

generated by the chanting of the mostly naked men in the circle that wasn't a circle. The ritual was coming to a crucial juncture, that much was clear, something was shimmering into view at the centre of that ladylike ellipse, just south of Monk Lewis, a bulky something, cylindrical in outline with a fluted dome on top, an entity from another plane of existence, from a terrible dimension.

'Dang!' shouted The Growl, as loud as he could. He had to break the taut cord of inevitability that was dragging the spell along. But the naked men kept chanting. Only Monk Lewis noticed.

The portly fellow looked up and saw them. He frowned as he did so, then his arms rose high and he began croaking strange words. He was rushing along the spell, The Growl realised, getting it done quicker, aiding the being that was materialising in the circle to enter the world slicker, the way a doctor might pull on a newborn baby's head with tongs. Monk Lewis' words were tongs, his tongue worked their handles, and The Growl understood that the creature that looked like a cylinder would obliterate them as soon as Monk Lewis instructed it to. For it was a demon of destruction.

There was no time to be lost. The Growl aimed carefully and squeezed the trigger of his gun. The report of the firearm in the narrow confines of the cellar was deafening. The bullet took off the scrotum of the nearest chanting man and rebounded into the pelvis of the next chanting man. The Growl fired again and again, emptying the chamber of his Colt.

Six bullets but thirteen scrotum strikes. Monk Lewis was the only one who retained his balls. Jorge clutched at The Growl and roared, 'Why did you shoot them *there*? Why not in the head?'

'Messing up the spell was my first concern.'

'And did you succeed?'

'Hark!' cried The Growl, and Jorge listened.

The original chant had been a deep bass rumble, felt in every nerve, bone and ligament of one's being. The new chant was high pitched, soprano, and it wasn't what the spell required.

The Chanters doubled over in agony. Their howls of pain were added to the chant. The Growl and Jorge winced.

The cylindrical entity in the ellipse changed shape. It shrank, withered and curled up. Monk Lewis screamed his frustration. The Chanters kept chanting but it was a piercing song now, ugly rather than intimidating. The half-formed being considered that they had cheated it.

Instead of blaming The Growl, it evidently considered the naked men to be traitors of some sort, or at least incompetents, and it decided to vent its anger on them. Although it was dwindling at every moment, it was still powerful enough to strike at the thirteen cowled individuals doubled over in that occult oval. Like an arthritic snake it straightened itself and lunged, one castrated cultist at a time, venom flowing from obsidian fangs.

The Chanters collapsed in convulsions and when

the final one was floored and the song had stopped, the demon also convulsed and disintegrated. Poison, blood and shot-off flesh turned the cellar into a grotesque death pit. The Growl nodded to himself. 'Good riddance.'

Monk Lewis was looking around the cellar in desperation, There was only one exit and it was blocked by these two intruders who had destroyed his cult in just a few minutes. The Growl started to reload his gun, but Jorge snarled, 'This fella's mine,' and he walked towards him. The knife was in his hand and a grin of triumph creased his mutilated face.

'Wait!' barked The Growl. 'I need him alive. I wasn't loading my gun to shoot him. Don't kill him just yet.'

But Jorge had reached Monk Lewis and had lunged to grab him by one of the tufts of hair on his tonsure. He pulled and to his surprise the head came off. It wasn't a real head after all, but a cowl, a cowl designed to *look* like a tonsured head. The real tonsured head was beneath. Jorge lifted his knife and prepared to plunge it. His arm was restrained.

The Growl was holding onto his knife arm, preventing him from plunging the blade into Monk Lewis.

'What's the meaning of this, señor?'

'I need him alive.'

'Why so? He's a villain and a diabolist.'

The Growl explained:

'He can give me information. I can force him to

use his magical powers to locate Traven for me. If you kill him now, I won't be able to do that. It will put me at a considerable disadvantage.'

'You said my revenge was more important.'

'Maybe I did, pard.'

'But what?' Jorge's eyes flashed with fury.

'I changed my mind.'

'You dog!' shouted Jorge, not fully aware of the aptness of the insult. 'I'll not let you deprive me of justice. How dare you tell me to practise restraint now I'm face to face with this murderer and mutilator! I will carve him into pieces, I promise, and you'll not stop me.'

'I will stop you,' said The Growl calmly.

Jorge turned purple.

'Cojones! Then we must fight a duel, you and I. My honour is at stake, the honour of my face, a face which was given to me by my family. The honour is therefore that of my family's face!

'Logical,' said The Growl, but his tone was sad.

'Knife or gun? Choose!'

The Growl sighed. He knew that nothing he could say would prevent Jorge from fighting this duel. His blood was on fire and he wasn't thinking straight, or rather he was thinking as straight as a horse ride through the pampas, which can create a very undulating route. That was his background, his culture, his origins, and he was fully conditioned by them. It didn't matter that he had regarded The Growl as a comrade. Honour was at stake and when honour is at stake for such a man, it's always the kind of stake that's well-done. For Jorge, this wasn't a risk, it was the stuff of life itself.

'Gun,' said The Growl at long last.

'One or two, eh?'

'Well, one each, I suppose.'

'We will fight the duel here and now,' said Jorge, 'and if I win, I will kill this monk. If you win, you can keep him alive for the purposes of extracting the information you require. Ready?'

'And if it's a draw?' wondered The Growl.

'Then life is a bitch.'

'Death too, one would have thought.'

'Enough talk! Fight!'

Jorge drew his revolver and he was fast. The Growl was faster. He thought that maybe he could just wound Jorge, put him out of action, rather than killing him, and so he aimed for Jorge's hand, the one that held the gun. But Jorge was performing a curious combat move.

He was leaping into the air and slightly to the side. Unfortunately his body entered the path of The Growl's bullet. He didn't even get a chance to squeeze his own trigger. He landed with a thud. The Growl cried out in dismay, but his distress wasn't so acute that he didn't notice Monk Lewis trying to make a run for it. Turning, he seized the sorcerer by the scruff and shook him until he went limp. The Growl was beyond fury.

'His death is *your* fault.'

Monk Lewis spat, 'You are the one who shot him.'

'Only with a bullet.'

The Growl released him and he slumped.

'You shot him with a chain of circumstances, with cause and effect,' he said, as he prodded Monk Lewis with the toe of his boot. 'Now let me explain what I'm going to do with you.'

He beckoned for Monk Lewis to stand.

'I'm not going to torture you, unless you refuse to assist me. I want you to use your occult powers to locate a man for me. His name is Traven. I have extra sensitivity to supernatural activity, so if you only pretend to use magical powers to track him down, I will know.'

'Traven is familiar to me,' said Monk Lewis.

'Really? How's that?'

'He briefly joined The Chanters when he arrived in Loreto and took part in a few of our rituals, but a deep commitment to occultism held no appeal for him. He went off somewhere one day.'

'Right, and now I want you to tell me where.'

'What if I refuse?'

'It will be very bad for you, pard.'

'Will you cut off my ears?' cried Monk Lewis. He quietly put his cowl on and it covered most of his head.

'What use would I have for them?'

'I don't know. Some ruffian types collect them, I guess. This world is mad. I am not such a bad person really.'

'They all say that. Even the worst murderer reckons he's a nice fella deep down, but all that's subjective, it don't amount to a hill of has-beans, get it? And you have been wickedly cavorting.'

Monk Lewis blushed in the recesses of his cowl.

'With devils,' added The Growl.

'I do what I must in order to survive and grow,' said Monk Lewis quietly, and he began sobbing, but his eyes were barely visible thanks to the shadows of his cowl, even though the cowl itself was painted to resemble his own head. The painted eyes were dry, mocking.

The Growl pondered. From close up, the cowl of Monk Lewis looked like a cowl. Only from a distance did it look like a tonsured man, like the tonsured man who was wearing it, in fact.

A mask in the shape of your own face is a peculiar sort of mask, decided The Growl. There was something inherently unhealthy about it. As he thought these thoughts, Monk Lewis recovered and said, 'I will do as you ask. It's not a difficult spell. I will perform it.'

'Not difficult for you, maybe,' corrected The Growl.

'You also know magic.'

'You can tell that, can you? Well, the kind of magic I know ain't black or white but sort of neutral. And it's not very powerful because I am only a novice despite my months of study in a cave.'

'Months are never sufficient. Even years are inadequate. It takes *decades* to become an authentic sorcerer.'

'I gathered that. But proceed with the spell.'

Monk Lewis nodded.

He stepped back a few paces, raised his arms, muttered words in a tongue unknown to The Growl and possibly to Monk Lewis himself. Then he stood on one leg and revolved slowly, struggling to keep his balance. At the same time he extended one of his arms to its maximum length and pointed the index finger on the hand of that arm. The Growl watched all this in amazement, spellbound, for want of a better word, entranced.

The index finger began glowing, pulsing with an eerie red light. This glow was strongest when Monk Lewis was facing the south during his slow rotation on one leg. The Growl realised that he was acting like a direction finder, some sort of organic compass. He cried:

'South it is then!'

Monk Lewis stopped revolving. He was a little dizzy. He said, 'Yes, but I learned more than that. The spell enabled me to see with my mind what Traven is doing. I know his activities as well as his whereabouts. Promise not to kill me and I will tell you everything!'

The Growl sighed. He didn't like the idea of setting Monk Lewis free, but when he made a promise he almost never broke it. The information would be a great asset to his quest. He said:

'Very well, I promise. But no funny tricks.'

'How about serious tricks?'

'None of those, either. If you play any sort of trick at all, my promise will break and then I will shoot you.'

Monk Lewis digested this, then he said, 'I learned from the spirits that are floating all around us in the aether that the man named Traven is now part of a new gang smuggling weapons across the sea to rebels in Sinaloa. He is waiting with a shipment down south.'

'Where exactly down south?'

'On a little deserted island named Cayo, which is near to the much bigger island of San José, also semi-arid. Not too many people live down in that part of Baja. It's a good place to conduct smuggling operations. Now I have told you all this, will you let me go free?'

'Not just yet,' replied The Growl.

'But why not?'

'You're coming with me.'

'I can't tell you anything more than I already have.'

The Growl shook his head.

'No longer require you for information. I need you for insurance purposes. Safer for me if you're a hostage.'

Monk Lewis began sobbing again. Tears squirted from under his cowl and this time The Growl laughed at them.

The Growl had taken Monk Lewis hostage and they had found a small boat for sale in the harbour and The Growl had paid for it. Now they were sailing down the eastern coast of Baja towards Cayo island, the rendezvous point where the rebels were going to pick up the guns.

It was a dramatic coastline with mountains to starboard and sea to port, a sea full of whales and dolphins. An obscure part of the world, sure enough, an offshoot of Mexico, a peninsula that for centuries was thought to be an island and on which many ships were wrecked.

Thinking about wrecks made The Growl brood over the wrecked face of Jorge and the futility of the duel. But that was life, a tragic comedy, and it was to be hoped that maybe in the future things wouldn't be like this. They would be better, more equitable, kinder, happier.

Monk Lewis resented being a hostage. He answered when spoken to, but otherwise remained withdrawn, keeping his real features concealed in his cowl, which was no longer as effective as it had been in creating the illusion of a head thanks to the erosive qualities of the sea spray. The water that lashed them had worn away much of the painted design.

The Growl tried to enjoy the voyage and he partly did. But he was cautious too, wary, even tense, and this was right. Thanks to his extra sensitivity to occult forces, he doubted very much that Monk Lewis would attempt anything rash. It would be suicide for the portly occultist.

They both knew this and the journey was uneventful.

But The Growl had to forego sleep. He wouldn't put it past Monk Lewis to try to stab him or strangle him if he lost consciousness. Not that he had a knife or a cord, nor was he strong, but The Growl had lost strength too, by using his power to detect supernatural activity.

They carefully sailed through the narrow channel between two islands, the Isla Carmen and the Isla Danzante, both uninhabited. Most of the islands off the coast of Baja, on both sides of the peninsula, appeared to be uninhabited. It was the perfect hangout for outlaws, bandits, pirates and all the colourful scum that populated and disrupted more ordinary parts of the globe. And that is why The Chanters had gone there, and Traven too, and why The Growl was there now, a case of the strange chasing the weird.

From Loreto to Cayo was about 150 miles, according to Monk Lewis, and the boat they were on was making about 4 knots, which means that it would be a voyage of about thirty-three hours.

The Growl would have to stay alert for the whole of that duration. To kill Monk Lewis and dump his body overboard occurred to him as an option, but it would bother him that he'd broken his promise. A terribly inconvenient thing to have principles in such a wild world!

Seals approached the boat and The Growl barked at them, not in an angry manner but a friendly one, and they barked back. It was almost a conversation, for seals and dogs are very similar in many ways.

Monk Lewis watched all this with a scowl on his half-hidden face.

They passed another island on their port side, Isla Monserrate, and later the Isla Santa Catalina. Then it was just the Isla Santa Cruz to pass before reaching the Isla San José. The tiny island of Cayo was on the south side of San José, an elongated strip of barren rocks, apparently studded with caves and covered with chains. These chains were a mystery.

Nobody knew what their function was or who had placed them there. They were rusty and massive. Many years later, long after The Growl had died and all the people he ever met were dead too, John Steinbeck visited the island and saw the chains with his own eyes. He wrote about them in his book, *The Log From the Sea of Cortez*, and he was baffled.

The island has since been renamed. It is no longer called Cayo but Lobos. The chains remain unexplained, though many have rusted through and fallen into the sea, where they confuse crabs.

The Growl shook Monk Lewis awake. The portly occultist groaned and opened his eyes and rearranged his cowl, which had slipped sideways during his sleep. He spoke drowsily, 'Huh? What?'

'We have reached Cayo,' said The Growl.

He pointed to indicate the thin line of the elongated island in the distance. This was the isolated rendezvous point the rebels had chosen.

Traven would be on the island right now, waiting.

The rebels would come across the Gulf from Sinaloa, pick up the guns and return across the sea. Then they would launch a raid on the capital to overthrow the regime. That, at least, was the plan.

'I am going to wait until dark to approach the island.'

'No!' cried Monk Lewis.

'Why not?' growled The Growl.

'The rocks! The submerged hazards! The spirits of the aether warned me. The cliffs are mostly sheer. There's only one safe approach on the western side, midway along the length of the island. You won't be able to steer safely if it is dark. Better to approach immediately.'

The Growl considered this. 'But Traven will see our approach and landing. I will lose the element of surprise.'

Monk Lewis shrugged. 'None of my business.'

An idea struck The Growl.

'Does he know what kind of boat the rebels have?'

'No,' admitted Monk Lewis.

'So maybe it looks exactly like this one?'

Monk Lewis nodded.

The Growl made a decision. He would attempt a landing now. They neared Cayo and it soon became clear that a man was waiting on the ridge that ran like a crease the length of the island.

That must be Traven, one of the six or seven or eight or nine murderers of his former boss, Ridley

Smart.

The Growl would get them all eventually.

Traven was the first.

The man on the ridge waved at them. The Growl waved back. Boats rarely attempted a landing on Cayo. No wonder Traven thought the rebels had arrived a little early to pick up the weapons!

The hull of the boat scraped against submerged rocks and The Growl was compelled to pull the tiller one way and then another in order to weave between these mostly hidden hazards.

But at last he found a small inlet and aimed the boat for it. Thanks to their momentum they rolled over the loose pebbles of a very narrow beach and came to a halt. The Growl jumped out.

'I'll get her secured by a rope. You wait here. He knows you and I don't want him to recognise you. We are supposed to be the rebels he is expecting. OK, now I've moored her.'

'Her?' gasped Monk Lewis.

'The boat,' said The Growl in surprise.

'Oh! Are boats female then? I thought you were talking about some girl I wasn't able to see. It's normal in my line of work to secure women with ropes. That explains the misunderstanding.'

'Your *line* of work? Is that supposed to be a joke? You don't work. Spells and demons aren't proper work.'

'What are they then?' Monk Lewis was offended.

'A hobby,' said The Growl.

The occultist pouted but his pout was concealed

by his cowl. The Growl adjusted his own cowl and set off.

He began climbing the cliffs on a very precarious path. In his eagerness he had forgotten to tie up Monk Lewis.

That was a mistake!

The occultist snarled to himself and he stared at the chains that festooned the island with fascination. They were very long and the links were large. The fact he didn't know what they were for was irrelevant. They would still obey a skilled sorcerer. He inhaled deeply, raised his arms, breathed out, twisted his face into the likeness of a goblin.

Then he started chanting, his eyes bulging as he did so, his body shaking and drool pouring from his mouth.

Casting a spell with a monophonic chant wasn't easy. It would have been better for him if The Chanters were there, but they were all dead, slain by the horrible entity they had been conjuring up in the cellar of that house in Loreto. He would have to make do without them. And he was capable of doing that, he was very experienced and skilled.

His face in the shadows of his cowl purpled and his chant turned into half a death rattle. Perspiration trickled down his chin. The strain was immense but the effort was worth it. The chains bolted to the cliffs nearest him began to stir, then other chains started to move too.

They rattled dully as they twisted and swung.

They were like serpents that had woken up after a long hibernation. Monk Lewis kept chanting. That was an essential part of the ritual. His arms waved in the air, describing weird symbols and eldritch geometrical patterns.

The Growl was still climbing the path. He hadn't yet noticed the moving chains. He was concentrating on reaching the top. He did so and Traven stood waiting to greet him. Traven still didn't realise that The Growl wasn't a rebel. He smiled and extended his hand.

'I been standing here on the ridge so I could see you coming, but I left the guns in a cave at the base of the cliff,' he said, and when he realised that there was a murderous intent in the stance of The Growl, he added, 'Hey what's up? You planning a double-cross?'

'Just a single cross,' answered The Growl.

'What does that mean?'

'It means you killed my friend, Ridley Smart, and I been trailin' you and now I have caught you. Get it?'

Traven grinned. He was unbothered by the unpleasant surprise. He was a desperado who always expected the unexpected. He said, 'Sure, I understand. So what happens next, amigo?'

'A whoopin', I reckon,' said the amigo.

'With bare hands, huh?'

The Growl shook his cowled head.

'Seems we're going to have a shoot-out right here on an island that's the most barren godforsaken place I ever seen. I see you got a Colt in a holster on your belt. I don't need a holster.'

'Keep your six-shooter up your butt?'

The Growl snarled.

He raised his gloved left hand and his gun appeared in it as if by magic. A conjuror's trick but a practical one.

'Draw,' said The Growl, as his eyes blazed.

Traven saw the chain first.

It was sneaking and snaking up behind The Growl. Suddenly it lunged for his leg and almost coiled around it. But the reactions of the dog-man were too fast for it. The chain was rusty and slow as a consequence. The Growl leaped to the side, whirled and ducked. At the same time, Traven drew his gun and fired a shot at The Growl, narrowly missing him. The bullet whizzed past his shoulder and took some shirt fabric with it.

More chains approached from all sides.

'Monk Lewis, damn his hide!' cried The Growl. He acrobatically dodged the lashing chains while also taking care to make himself an impossible target for Traven. The chains ignored Traven. The spell had specified that he wasn't to be harmed. Some of the chains tied themselves into nooses and tried to snatch The Growl, others acted like mighty whips and bashed at the ridge, knocking a chunk of rock off with each strike.

The rock shrapnel was as hazardous as bullets.

The Growl was exhausted.

But he kept his head and summoned up all his

reserves of energy. Slowly but surely he was approaching Traven. Sometimes he would have to jump back a step or two, often he went sideways, but the general progression was always closer to his enemy. Traven fired again and The Growl ducked and the bullet ricocheted off a chain. The Growl dodged the ricochet too, jumped, bounded, rolled, pranced, skipped, capered.

Monk Lewis was still chanting for all he was worth, his throat burning, a rictus look on his face. But The Growl was unaware of the agonies he endured to keep the spell active. All he knew was that Traven was almost within reach. Another gymnastic roll and bounce and now he had that villain in a headlock and was twisting his head around.

Traven knew he planned to break his neck.

He had learned a little magic during his association with The Chanters, a few spells at a very low level. He couldn't make these chains come alive, as Monk Lewis had, but now they were moving he could direct them, assist them by reinforcing their instructions.

He knew enough to do that. In desperation, he reached into his mind and achieved the desired psychological state, despite the stress he was under from The Growl's headlock, and cried:

'Kill the man in the cowl. Kill him now!'

The chains heard him.

Traven thought that this order would be the end of The Growl, but Monk Lewis was also wearing a cowl. The chains weren't bright enough to know the difference. For them it was all part of a strange day's work. They reached out to the boat and four of them seized Monk Lewis, one around each of his limbs. He stopped chanting and screamed.

With the end of his chant, the spell was broken but the chains didn't stop moving just yet. They still had some momentum, that's why. They lifted Monk Lewis high in the air and then they all pulled in different directions. His arms and his legs came off with a horrible sucking sound and his limbless torso fell onto the pebbles of the beach with a fruity splat. He was still screaming but his scream had less power in it now.

Only then did all the chains cease moving and resume their former inert positions. Traven was peering over the edge of the ridge in disbelief, shouting down at Monk Lewis to get up.

'He can't. He doesn't have any feet.'

Traven whirled around.

The Growl pushed him with the index finger of a gloved hand. Traven lost his balance but windmilled his arms in an attempt to remain upright. It was no good. He tipped over and plummeted off the cliff. He landed on Monk Lewis, who was trying to wriggle out of the way, and the fruity splat was louder this second time. The Growl nodded.

'Like a banana falling on a melon …'

He rested a minute.

Then he made his way down the steep path to

the boat. Monk Lewis was dead and so was Traven. His quest had been a success. He was still upset about his friend, Jorge, but all in all, everything had worked out fine. He peered inside the nearest cave and saw wooden boxes piled high. The guns intended for the rebels. He took one of the boxes with him and stored it in the boat. The rebels could have the others, if they liked.

He had no opinion about their political cause, it was none of his business, but one crate of weapons would be useful to him. He could sell them. He was running low on funds and he wanted to get on the trail of the other killers of Ridley Smart. Those killers could be anywhere but were probably back in the United States. There was one less now but what did that mean? He must make sure all of them were stone dead.

Stone dead, yeah. Traven had expired not on impact with the rocks of the beach but the stomach of an occultist. He might have expected a soft landing on such a generous belly but there's a thing called physics. When an object falls, its potential energy gets converted into kinetic energy, and when it hits something that kinetic energy is converted into damage. Traven was a mass of bruises and blood, Monk Lewis was just a mess.

The Growl pushed the boat into the water and jumped into her. He would sail due east across the Gulf to the Mexican mainland and make his way to the nearest city, which happened to be Culiacán, and sell the guns there. He knew they would fetch a good price. Then he would head north and cross the border into Arizona or Texas. It would take a few weeks, yes, but that was acceptable. He was an extremely patient fella.

Scrub that. He was a patient man-dog.

As the boat sailed out onto the belly of the sea, he thought about his earlier encounter with the bandit in the diving suit. His meditation in the cave enabled him to be extra sensitive to occult vibrations. It had given him a greater *insight* into supernatural stirrings. It was still exhausting for him and also he needed to come up for the 'air' of normality. Yet if he wore a diving suit on this insight, he'd be able to explore deeper into the oceans of occult thoughts without a need to surface for that air. But how to build a diving suit for an insight? It wasn't too hard a problem to solve, he judged.

He would solve it. In the meantime, adios!

Chapter Four
Dog Face Chief

He crept through the long grass of the plains and he raised his head occasionally to sniff the air. Yes, he caught the scent again. The prey he was hunting was a few miles ahead. His tongue lolled with anticipation. He had been lucky and it must be admitted that luck was the one factor he couldn't do much about. Magic was an art, not a science, and chance played a part in the way things worked out. His ears pricked up and he growled.

It was a very low growl, for his own benefit, out there on the endless wide expanse of gently undulating grasslands. He was in Kansas and he had learned it wasn't the flattest state after all. True, the hills were mostly gentle, but what did that matter? His savagery would cancel out all the gentleness he found here. His fangs were bared. He had a mission to accomplish and it was one that required a merciless nature. The call of the wild.

He was going to kill the killer of his friend. It was that simple. And yes, he was part dog. He had the brains and wisdom of a veteran male during one of the roughest periods in his nation's history, the experience and the stamina, but his ferocity, determination and courage were wholly canine. He was fast and brutal, yet at heart he was a good person, generous and thoughtful. Many had come to him and he had usually helped them.

It was an unhappy combination of unavoidable circumstances that had led him to this present moment. Fate liked to play tricks, that's all, and some of the tricks were cruel. But he knew what had happened and he knew what he should do about it. He had a duty, a moral duty, and it was a question of honour. But it was more than this too. He was an agent of justice, preventative justice at that, an emissary of correctness and truth.

The killer was ahead, resting his horse, sitting on the grass as he did so, a pleasant place to pass the time in idleness. Not all killers looked like fugitives and this one didn't. That was the strange thing about good and evil. The purest beings were often plain, the most corrupt ones were frequently alluring, and it was easy to forget that appearances mean nothing. But he wouldn't forget the facts in a hurry. His friend was dead.

A horrid murder, unprovoked, and he was the avenger. It often happens, he told himself. But if he didn't kill his friend's killer, there was no telling what the killer would do next. Maybe kill another of his friends. Better to end everything neatly. Just another fifty yards and he would be able to pounce on his target. He raised his head one more time, sniffed.

The scent was strong. The horse scent was

powerful but the killer's odour was even more pungent. He hadn't washed for a long time, it seemed. Well, that was nothing out of the ordinary here. Soon enough, he would be washed in his own blood anyway, and after that he would never need to bathe again. He felt in his pockets for the two small jars that he carried. Yes, they were still there. The powder of life and the powder of death.

Twenty yards. Now he must slither the final distance even more carefully. The horse's ears pricked up. He held his breath. The horse returned to nibbling the tall grass. Another yard on his belly. His victim hadn't noticed anything at all yet. He was sitting with his back to his assassin, whistling a low tune, happy to be doing nothing in the fertile flat lands. Nothing can be beautiful, and soon he would be nothing himself. Watch!

The Growl had sailed from Cayo across the Gulf of California to the shores of the Mexican state called Sinaloa. An enjoyable voyage on the waters of a calm sea full of big playful whales.

He landed on a deserted stretch of coastline and left the boat on the beach for anyone who came along and wanted her. With the crate of guns balanced on his shoulder he slowly made his way inland to Culiacán, which was the nearest town of any size in the region.

It wasn't far. He was lucky enough to find a buyer for the weapons within a few hours of his arrival. He pocketed the silver coins and went for a meal and a drink in a bar. He wouldn't stay in Culiacán long. He wanted to head back to the USA, where the men he was hunting were more likely to be. The following day he set off, north and a little east.

He was extra sensitive to occult vibrations but when it came to detecting the presence of a normal man, he had to rely on his natural senses, though his hearing, smell and taste were far more acute than when he had been plain Bill Bones, a newspaperman in St Louis. He now had most of the abilities of a dog and he intended to use them fully.

It wasn't a question of sniffing the base of every cactus he encountered, to see if any of the men he was after had passed this way. It didn't work like that. He didn't even know who the men he was hunting *were*. And they didn't know who he was, or even that he was pursuing them. He wasn't even certain of their exact number. It might be five, six, seven or eight. All he knew was that it was now one less than what it had been.

One *less* or one *fewer*? That was a grammatical question that confused him still, despite his experience as a newspaperman. He shook it out of his head. He could teach himself the finer points of the language later. The main thing was to kill the killers of his friend, one by one or all together if necessary, the killers of Ridley Smart, assuming he could find them. And if he didn't find them? It was no big deal really. The main thing is that he would have *tried*. He recalled what his shaman had taught him once:

To try is almost equivalent to actually doing. Yes, and his experiences since had confirmed this in some ways, denied it in others. For instance, The Lord had tried to destroy the White House but had failed. Did this mean the White House had been obliterated anyway? What of Monk Lewis, who had tried to conjure a demon that resembled a phallus? He had failed too. But did the fact he had tried mean the demon was barging around somewhere on Earth? The question was an intricate one, not easy to answer.

The days passed and he left Mexico and crossed the Rio Grande into Texas on an old wooden hand-operated cable ferry that was just large enough for one foot passenger and one horse. In Texas he made his way to San Antonio. That's where he hung around for a couple of weeks. In a saloon one night he picked up a clue as to the whereabouts of another of the killers he was seeking. The fella in question was holed up in Kansas.

The Growl left San Antonio at dawn of the next day and rode due north for weeks, crossing first into Oklahoma and then passing through that state and over the border into Kansas. That's where he was now, deep in the grasslands, and he was very close to catching the killer.

Yes, he was close to catching the killer. Ten yards away. Time to pounce. There was tremendous energy in his back legs. He tensed and launched himself at his target and as he did so he growled.

He should have landed on his victim, his teeth fixed on his neck. But to his amazement, the fella had moved, rolling out of the way. The avenger landed on the ground, bounded up at once, his jaws still wide and found himself facing the barrel of a drawn gun. He cried:

'Bill Bones, I have come far for you!'

The other replied:

'Ain't my name. I'm just The Growl.'

'You killed my friend.'

'No, that can't be true. You are mistaken.'

'I am never wrong.'

'A mighty big claim, pard. Who are you?'

'Can't you work it out?'

The Growl frowned and scrutinised his would-be assassin more carefully. He was startled by what he saw.

He was bewildered and befuddled. The hand that was holding the gun went limp. All the vitality in his body drained away. He was staring at his erstwhile mentor, the shaman who had taught him mind control, who had helped to turn him partly into a dog.

He mumbled, 'Tony?' almost in disbelief.

'Yeah, that's right.'

'What are you doing out of your cave?'

'Came looking for you.'

'But why? I was your pupil. Have I not done your teachings honour since I left the cave? Have I not been a *good* dog?'

'You killed my friend.'

'That can't be right. I am the one who is trailing the killer of my friend, not you. I am The Growl. You are Tony the Shaman. A fella who helped murder my former boss is a few miles ahead. He is unaware I am following him. I'm resting my horse ready for a final reckoning. He killed Ridley Smart and I don't know why. I intend to see justice done.'

'I happen to be in a similar position. You helped to kill my friend and you were unaware I was on your trail. The final reckoning is here already. Yes, you killed my friend and I don't know why.'

'Tony! What friend of yours did I kill? Sure, I have killed people since my transformation. But all were bad men, villains, sorcerers and maniacs. How can any of them be the friend you mean?'

'Bobby, that's who.'

The Growl shook his head. 'I never had any dealings with anyone by that name. You've made some errors.'

'Bobby the Shaman.'

The Growl shrugged helplessly. 'I still don't know who that is. Tony! You must believe me. I'm innocent.'

'No, you aren't. But I'm not surprised you don't really know what I mean. Bobby is still alive. But he will die in the future *because* of you. Not directly, I don't mean that you shot him or something. I can't read the future *precisely*, no one can do that, no matter how skilled in magic they are. But I know he will die thanks to your actions. And so –'

'You are obliged to take revenge on me?'

'Succinctly put, Bill.'

'But he isn't dead yet. So it's absurd to blame me. How far in the future is his death going to occur?'

'Ten years almost, I reckon.'

The Growl considered this. 'That means I will still be alive ten years in the future. How can you kill me now? That would create one of those paradoxes. It is all stuff and nonsense, Tony.'

'It is stuff, sure enough. I'm right with you there, Bill. But nonsense? That is where I am going to have to disagree with you. It isn't actually your presence that is required for the death of my friend Bobby. The culmination of a chain of events that you set into motion is enough. Understand? You did something quite recently that will lead to Bobby's death. That's why I have come for you. I plan to get revenge for him in advance!'

The Growl frowned at this and he felt utterly dejected. He had felt a deep affection and respect for the shaman who had taught him all he knew. The fact they were now enemies was awful.

'I am real sorry about all this, Tony.'

'Been trailin' you, Bill, just the same way you been trailin' the man ahead of you. But I got to you first.'

'Yes, you did,' admitted The Growl.

'And now –' Tony sighed.

'Not a shootout?' asked The Growl.

Tony smiled, his doglike face even hairier than

that of his former pupil. He was the doggiest of all shamans and he knew it. The Growl was half dog but his master was at least four-fifths canine.

'I don't need guns,' replied Tony. 'I have other methods. And I am going to give you a choice, Bill, which is more than what you gave destiny when you set up the conditions that would ultimately result in Bobby's doom. I have two small jars in my pockets, see?'

'Wait a minute, Tony! Just tell me first. How did I kill this friend of yours? This friend who isn't dead yet?'

'That question is easily answered. You trapped a woman called Jalamity Kane in his cave. That's what you did, Bill. She will study diligently with him for ten years and change into a unicorn.'

'That's astounding.'

'When those ten years are up, she will leave the cave. Bobby will follow her. She doesn't like being followed by anyone. She turns and chases him. He runs for the shelter of the cave but she is faster. Her horn is seven feet long. It goes right up his tush, Bill. Don't know how many feet of it go up. The future is quite hazy, a blur, but several feet.'

'Eh? Up the tush?'

'You know, the fundament. The black hole of jacksy.'

'The ole bumhole, huh?'

'That's right, Bill. The back alley, browneye, dung funnel, gump stump, poop chute, tooter, wazoo, where the sun don't shine, the rusty sheriff's badge, haemorrhoid highway. The rectum, my friend. Not the ideal way to vacate this existence, this vale of tears, is it?'

'But how am I responsible for that? Jalamity Kane is the one to blame. I never horned a man bumwise!'

'Mighty relieved to hear that, Bill, but it don't change anything. It's just a simple conceit of ordinary folks that an accidental cause and effect has nothing to do with them. The truth is that we all ought to be held accountable for every action that has a reaction. Get it?'

'I get it, sure, but I don't agree with it.'

'Why not, Bill?'

'Because I don't like it.'

Tony nodded and smiled. 'That's about the sum of it. We don't agree with things we don't like, and we tend not to like them when they don't suit us, and that's not a real objection to anything. I want you to imagine something, Bill. I want you to imagine you have been a shaman for five decades or more, living in a cave, meditating there in peace.'

'I can imagine that. I was with you for six months. It's just a hundred times longer than what I went through.'

'Right. So you are in that cave all alone. Then you accept a new pupil and teach her for ten years. At the end of that time she rams three, maybe three and a half, maybe even more, feet of unicorn horn up your butt and it's unlubricated. You've been celibate all your life and ain't prepared for that kinda thing. That's what poor Bobby endured on account of what you did. Or I should say, what he *will* endure. It ain't happened yet.'

The Growl puffed out his cheeks. 'I won't argue no more, Tony. Do what you think you must. But I won't go down without a fight. I know you have the powers of a full shaman and I don't. You can probably reduce me to ashes in a few seconds. But I won't surrender.'

Tony held up the two small jars he had brought with him. 'You must pick one, Bill. That's the vengeance.'

'What are they exactly?' asked The Growl.

Tony smiled rather sadly.

'The powder of instant death is in one. The powder of eternal life is in the other. If you choose the former, I'll throw it over you and your flesh dissolves in an instant. If you choose the latter, you will become immortal. Most men would choose the second jar, but they ain't thought it through properly. I'm hoping you will think about the matter deeply.'

'I will. In fact I am right now,' said The Growl.

'Tell me your conclusions.'

'The powder of instant death will end my life and then I'll have an eternity of rest. No more troubles. But the time hasn't come for me to enjoy my rest. The killers of Ridley Smart are still at large and I want to get them. I don't mind the prospect of dying, in fact I'll welcome it one day, but it's too soon. Tony. So the powder of instant death isn't right.'

'You choose the powder of eternal life?'

'Nope. That's just as bad or perhaps even worse. If I live forever, then I'll be able to kill the killers of my boss, but what happens after that? I'll be forced to continue forever, aimlessly indestructible. And one day the human race will come to an end, all animal life too, all plant life as well, but I'll still be around, the last living thing on the husk of a dead planet. Untold millions of years in the future. That's a horrible idea, Tony.'

'Which one do you choose then? You must choose one.'

'What if you mix 'em together?'

'Don't be absurd. That would be very weird and I have absolutely no idea what would happen if I did that. Quit stalling for time, Bill, and choose one. The chances of tricking me with guile are zero. I can sniff out a trick in a trice. Just choose one and be done with it, boy.'

The Growl nodded slowly, and then he chose.

The gun was in his gloved hand in a blink and he fired two shots in such quick succession that the second almost overtook the first. One bullet struck the little jar holding the powder of instant death and the other struck the little jar holding the powder of eternal life. Powder from both jars was thrown over the shaman and he coughed as it entered his lungs. Then his eyes bulged and something odd happened, something utterly terrible.

Tony's flesh dissolved. He turned to a skeleton and this skeleton fell apart and the bones clattered down like the rungs of a collapsing ladder upon the dirt and grass of the plain. But the bones remained alive. And now the skull part of Tony, which was the cranium of a dog, began rushing and seizing the bones in its jaws and trying to bury them in the soil, but it had no legs to do the digging. The femur bones were in its mouth.

The Growl thought this was a dreadful sight. He stepped forward, leaned over, snatched up a few bones and hurled them as far as he could. But the head of Tony saw this as a game and rushed after them, fleshless jaws snapping, with a silent bark in its mouth, retrieving them one by one and bringing them back. Somewhere else, the tail bones wagged in doggy delight. The dead shaman was a living skeleton, uncoordinated, atavistic, playful, and determined to bury the remnants of itself for future usage.

It even tried to bury itself, for it was made of bone.

The Growl shouted out:

'Stop this, Tony, please stop it. I never thought it was going to be this way. You shouldn't have brought those jars with you. It ain't right. It could have been done with guns. Just stop this now!'

But the scattered bones paid him no heed.

The skull continued to gather them and at one point it almost assembled a complete skeleton of the shaman. But then it broke them up. It moved over the ground by rolling at a fair lick of speed.

The Growl walked away.

He still didn't believe he was responsible for Bobby getting shafted by that unicorn horn. Jalamity ought to be blamed for that. Just her. He looked over his shoulder at the scuffling bones.

'I am the dog face chief!' he cried. 'Not you, Tony, but me, The Growl. I am the top dog now. Sorry, pard.'

Tears were trickling down his furry cheeks.

But he didn't waste time.

His horse was rested now and he jumped in the saddle and rode on. About two hours later he caught up with a fella named Smith, one of the gang that had murdered his boss, and he shot him. How many left now? The answer depended on an accurate count of the killers' numbers. A minimum of four remained but a maximum of seven. He would find them. He rode and he didn't bother to check what direction he was riding in.

When night fell, the moon came out.

He growled at it twice.

Once for himself and once for Tony.

And he was lonesome.

Chapter Five
The Cliché Hunter

The girl in a sumptuous dress made from luxurious curtains by one of her maids ran down the sweeping stairway to the ballroom. The musicians had tuned up and a dance was about to begin. The chandeliers sparkled. Her hair flowed like molten gold over her silvery shoulders. Her lips were carnelian and her mouth gleamed like a waxed carnation. Her eyes were blue. She was a Southern belle and she rang the changes with her soul.

She spoke with a drawl that was like a lilt, or maybe it was a lilt that was like a drawl, there wasn't enough time to work it out, because no sooner had she reached the bottom step of the stairway and started to speak than a man walked over to her and shot her in the chest. She collapsed without a sigh. There was a gasp of horror from the assembled dancers and other guests. The killer turned to face them with an ironic grin and said:

'She was a cliché and I'm a Cliché Hunter, that's my role in life. I am here to rid the entire country of clichés.'

The gun he held was a rifle but it had a very short barrel, no longer than a revolver's. Even as the words left his mouth, the barrel doubled in length. Now it was less peculiar to look upon. One of the men on the ballroom floor frowned at him and walked briskly forwards.

'You have murdered a lady, you venomous scoundrel, and now I intend to do away with you. Say your prayers!'

The Cliché Hunter rolled his eyes. 'An honourable young man, avenger of beauty, yet another cliché. How appalling. I said my prayers before I came here, dear boy, now please say yours …'

And he shot the individual in the throat.

The barrel of his gun doubled in length again, and now it looked just like a normal rifle. He turned to leave, calling back over his shoulder, 'I ain't one for formalities. I am the Cliché Hunter but my name is Ned. Call me that when you turn tonight into a shocking anecdote.'

And off he went. No one followed him. They were too stunned. Not that it was unusual in the state of Mississippi for gunmen to gatecrash parties, causing trouble with bullets and leers. But this fella had seemed different, more like one of those religious fanatics than a desperado. The bodies of Harlot O'Scara and the young man who had come to the defence of her memory lay on the floor and leaked rather a lot. It was very messy.

But Ned was safely ensconced in the night, safely for him, sure, but not for any man or woman who happened to be passing and was a cliché in one way or another. The Cliché Hunter had hunted clichés in his mind for decades, but only now had he started the task for real.

He planned to visit every square inch of land in the United States, wiping out as many clichés as he could find on the way. There was no good reason he couldn't make clichés extinct eventually. And then the world would be a better place. Originality would flourish.

As for his gun, he had obtained it in a very peculiar shop in New Orleans from a very strange man who had called himself Gunsmith Ghouls. That wasn't so important really. What mattered is that it grew longer every time he erased a cliché and when it grew longer its range and accuracy increased. His smile also doubled in intensity with each kill.

'Goddam clichés, how I loathe each sonofabitch!'

He loped through the gloom.

Mississippi had seemed like a good place to begin his campaign. He could travel up and down the river on one of the paddle boats, shooting minstrels who did the same old acts, assassinating gamblers who palmed cards. Ned Parker, his full name was, and he was the son of Presbyterian immigrants from Ruritania or some such place, a land overseas at any rate. They had brought him up strictly, with many clichés, but he'd rebelled.

'Spare the rod and spoil the child,' they had said.

A favourite quotation.

As a result, they never loaned any of their rods to any neighbour who was in dire need of one. They had plenty of them, a house full of rods, wooden and iron and ceramic rods, serving no purpose whatsoever. A neighbour might call and say, 'I've got this new threshing machine, steam powered, but it's missing one of the connecting rods, a camshaft. I see you have lots of rods. Could you spare one to help me out, please?'

And they would shake their sombre heads and point to Ned. 'He is a child and if we spare a rod, he'll go rotten. That's what the good book says. Fungus will envelop him and he'll spoil.'

'I don't think it quite means that,' the neighbour would protest, but Ned's parents would glower at him fiercely.

'Heretic! Heathen!'

'Those are two different things,' the neighbour would point out. 'A heretic and a heathen aren't synonymous.'

'Pagan! Idolator! Onanist! If we spare the rod, the child will spoil. There's not much use in a fungoidal child.'

'OK, get a grip, don't lose your heads over it.'

'Begone, ye diabolist!'

And that was the environment Ned had been raised in, but just a few weeks shy of his fifteenth birthday he'd skipped home and never came back. He got a job in a travelling carnival as a sword swallower's assistant. He learned how to swallow swords himself too. Then he ran off to New York and secured himself employment as an umbrella stand in the lobby of a lawyer's office, swallowing the umbrellas as if they were rapiers.

Six months later he was on the road again, heading west to California, the journey teaching him many skills. He worked on the railroads first, then later as a prospector, peach picker, huckster, shyster, climatologist, blacksmith, dentist's model, deputy sheriff, dishwasher in a restaurant, card sharp in a blunt saloon, a host of dead end jobs, including duck impersonator. He went north to Canada, then to Alaska too, eventually across to Quebec, back down to Texas, all across the continent, looking for his purpose.

He found it in New Orleans. It was carnival time and the dancers dressed in elaborate costumes were cavorting and twirling, whirling and capering, and some of them were even hyperventilating. Ned felt suffused with a weird energy and he skipped along as he walked.

Down a narrow side street he chanced on the shop that was to give him a reason for living, a meaning to existence, a mission of his own. Something in the window caught his eye, a rifle with the shortest barrel he'd ever seen, not much longer than a squonk's thumb.

He went inside and when he pushed the door it sounded a set of bells that chimed a deeply disturbing melody. The shop was cluttered, overflowing with such a variety of curios and relics that he had difficulty picking his way to the counter, which was also piled high with knick-knacks and ornaments. It was a shop that reeked of ancient death.

But there was a figure behind the counter, a short man whose head barely rose above the level of the books, tools and miscellaneous items that were all jumbled together. He bowed a greeting, slamming his forehead onto one of the few clear patches on the counter.

The sound it made was like a drum.

He said, 'Welcome.'

Ned nodded in response and gazed around. Then he said, 'Interested in the gun in the window. What is it?'

The little man opened a hatch in the base of the counter and came out. Ned saw that he was about four feet high but wore platform shoes that added another foot in both senses of the word, a foot in height and a third foot that came off his normal left foot at a tangent. This was weird enough, but even weirder was the tooth that jutted from his mouth.

It was a fang and was so terrifically long it came down almost to the floor. It was multicoloured too, striped in fact, white and yellow and brown, like some sort of insane barber's pole. It was very sharp at the end, a stiletto, and it could do a lot of damage if required. The exhaled breath of the little man smelled very strongly of vanilla. Ned was uncertain, frightened even, but he was too intrigued by the gun to leave. The little man introduced himself as Gunsmith Ghouls and then he said in a rich baritone:

'The gun in the window has chosen you. I will

give it to you for free. But you must do the work it wants.'

Without fully understanding, Ned nodded.

'I agree,' he replied.

Gunsmith Ghouls grinned and said, 'Good!'

Then he closed his eyes and his fang lost exactly half its length. It seemed to retract into his mouth. Now it came down only to the middle of his stomach. He opened his eyes and smiled.

'Every time I make a sale, that happens.'

'But I ain't paying.'

'There are other ways of paying. You will do what the gun wants, which is also what you want, deep down.'

'And that counts as payment, does it?'

'Sure,' said Gunsmith Ghouls. He dipped through the hatch, emerging on the far side of the counter. The books balanced on the surface wobbled. Ned was supposed to leave now, that much was obvious. He went to the window, picked up the gun and then walked out.

The chimes sounded and he realised he was trembling, but whether with an attack of anxiety or with relief, he couldn't say. He left New Orleans and ended up in Mississippi and on that journey he decided what the gun needed. It was an easy question when he asked what he himself needed. They would be the same thing, the shopkeeper had claimed.

That was when he decided to become a Cliché Hunter, *The* Cliché Hunter in fact, as there were no others. He was unique. That was significant and helped him to feel secure in his own flesh.

The daughter of a rich plantation owner, the walking cliché known to her family and friends as Harlot O'Scara, had been his first victim, the young hero who belatedly came to her aid was his second. Each time he killed a cliché, the barrel of his rifle would double in length, just as the fang of Gunsmith Ghouls halved every time *he* made a sale.

The two things were undoubtedly connected.

How? He couldn't say.

Nor did it matter much. It was simply magic.

Ned kept running.

His stride was easy, his muscles relaxed, his soul was tranquil. Yes, life is improved when one has a purpose.

In the following weeks he killed many other living clichés, including brash lawmen, verbose old-timers, snake oil salesmen. His rifle grew as long as one of those Kentucky rifles and then exceeded by far any gun in the world. One night he came across a cowboy making camp and eating beans. He had to shout to be heard, so far away was he, when the business end of the barrel of his gun was an inch away from the cowboy's head.

'Beans, eh? That's a cliché. Why do you people have to do such things? If you were cooking a lasagne or a pizza I would spare your life. But coffee and beans! It's time for you to die.'

'Whoever heard of a cowboy cooking pizza?'

'Exactly, my foolish friend.'

And Ned pulled the trigger and the cowboy was destroyed and the barrel of his gun doubled in length yet again.

Later that same month he encountered a wagon of pioneers headed west on the Oregon Trail and the patriarch of the family was dressed all in black and had a beard but no moustache and his wife wore a shawl and a bonnet and the words they spoke had a Biblical intonation.

Ned shot them and he didn't even need to be visible to them to do this. His rifle barrel was so long that he stood over the horizon, concealed by the rim of the world, and poked it into the wagon from afar, and it doubled in length with each fresh kill, removing him from the scene of the crime so that he no longer felt responsible for these murders.

On one occasion he shot a stealthy burglar who was in the act of climbing onto the roof of a bank. The burglar wore a mask and was an expert at picking locks and Ned picked him off, aware that he was a cliché but unaware that he'd just ended the life of Danny Bangs.

Once the most skilled burglar in the land.

Ned was utterly ruthless.

Eventually he tracked down his own father and mother and shot them too, because they were ageing clichés of the too-strict parental kind, and he stood in one state, in Indiana, while they remained in another, Ohio, and they died with no chance of even saying a prayer.

The story of his existence and exploits began to

spread by word of mouth and a little later by the printed word. Ballads were sung about this new legend, the Cliché Hunter, a man who hated unoriginality, and newspapermen scribbled articles speculating on his nature.

He shot a few of those newspapermen.

And now he sat on a stool in a depopulated part of Wyoming and reviewed his progress so far. The barrel of his gun was astoundingly long, testimony to a successful career in his chosen field.

His chosen field, in fact, was a barren rocky one, but a good place to enjoy a rest without being seen by people.

Wyoming was a state he particularly liked, and he had been all over, so his judgement was sound. But he felt it was important to steer clear of cities, towns and even the smallest settlements.

The last example of urbanity he'd experienced was in Casper, the friendly ghost town, almost in the centre of Wyoming, but surely it was a ghost town no longer. The inhabitants had fled because of a rumour of an invasion from space, from Venus or Mars or one of those other worlds up there. How gullible normal citizens are! They believe anything.

The day was coming to a close. The vast sky was darkening, the sun went down, the first stars came out. There was no moon but a cool breeze stirred the hairs on his head. He wore no hat because he didn't want to be a cliché. For the same reason he rode no horse, smoked no tobacco, gulped no whisky, catcalled no call girls, hitched no thumbs in his belt. He didn't even wear a belt, keeping his trousers up by willpower alone.

Ned Parker half closed his eyes and allowed the peace to bathe him. Then he felt the tickle of hot breath on his cheek. He was instantly alert, eyes wide, gazing up at a figure that wore a cowl. But he remained calm. He said, 'If I had a nickel for every tickle I ever felt –'

'How much would you have saved?'

'Nothin', I reckon.'

'Why not?' demanded The Growl.

Ned shrugged. 'Would have spent it all. But not on hard liquor or gambling or any of that nonsense. That's all a cliché. I might have spent it on something a man in this time and place would never be expected to purchase. One of those things ladies put ladders into.'

'Stockings, you mean?'

'Yeah, maybe, or possibly something else.'

'Are you Ned Parker?'

'That's right. Who's asking? And incidentally, why do you wear a cowl? It sorta makes you look like an owl. Say, that rhymes. I could be a poet and surely I would be, if it was no cliché.'

'*Surly*, you would be, did you say?'

'Surely, not surly.'

'Misheard you, which is pretty unusual, because my hearing is acute most of the time. Keen senses, see.'

'Just who the hell are you, stranger?'

The Growl explained:

'I've been seeking the killers of my former boss. A good friend as well as a boss, I should add. Recently I heard a rumour that three of them were hanging around this state. I looked and looked and finally found 'em playing cards in a shack on the wild slopes of the Beartooth Mountains. They were hiding out for a few months on account of some lawmen who were trailin' them, but I got to them first, unluckily for them.'

Ned shrugged. 'What business is that of mine?'

But The Growl continued:

'They had lost all the cards in the pack except one, which was the Ace of Spades, and they took turns playing it and passing it on, so all the games they played ended in a draw. And then I burst into the shack and *that* game ended in a draw too, but my draw was faster.'

'You shot them? I am hardly impressed. I have shot dozens of people in a short space of time. I am The Cliché Hunter and I am thinking that maybe you're some sort of cliché too. Am I right?'

The Growl pondered this question. 'Don't think so.'

'Your cowl is a monk's.'

'That doesn't mean a thing. Are monks clichés? And am I a monk? Chants would be a fine thing. But –'

Ned waited for the twist in the tale.

'You,' said The Growl.

'Me what? You ain't one of those annoying fellas who speak in riddles? I can't stand those scallywags.'

'You are the cliché,' announced The Growl.

'Oh yeah! And how?'

'The story of your exploits has spread. It has become a legend. One day it may turn into a myth. People will talk about The Cliché Hunter as if he is a part of universal culture. They will incorporate your identity into casual metaphors and similes. It's inevitable.'

'I don't like that,' admitted Ned.

'Then you know what to do, don't you? The rifle you are holding has the longest barrel of any gun in history. It stretches right around the world, almost, and back again. The business end is no more than a few inches from the back of your head. Squeeze the trigger, pard.'

Ned nodded. A solitary tear spilled from one eye.

The trigger was pulled.

There was a click followed by a blast, but Ned remained on his stool. The Growl looked down at him.

'The velocity of the bullet you have just discharged is 1400 feet per second and the diameter of the world at this latitude, which is about 43 degrees north, is something in the region of 18,000 miles. These figures ain't precise, but they're good enough for our purpose.'

Ned said, 'Eighteen thousand miles is 95,040,000 feet, which means it will take 67,886 seconds for the bullet to travel around the world and blow a hole in the back of my head. That's nineteen hours. Reckon

I'll just sit here and wait. I am a patient man. But tell me, my rifle barrel will double again once I am gone. What will you do with it then?'

'Hadn't thought about it. Maybe cut it up into lots of rods and donate it to a person who collects rods. Stop some innocent child spoiling. Allow me to put a pot of coffee on a fire to boil while you wait. I'll make the fire first and get a pot from somewhere. The nearest town is a six hour ride. I can get there and be back in twelve hours, leaving another seven hours in which to entertain you. Do you play chess? I can get a board.'

'Chess is a cliché. I much prefer mancala.'

'What's that, pard?'

'An African game, almost unknown over here. Rows of stones or nuts or beads and you sow them as you go along and it's pretty neat, but the truth of the matter is I just want to rest easy.'

'Sleep then. I'll wake you up in time for your death. That's really the most that anyone can do for a fella.'

'Tell me, what made you decide to come after me?'

'I'd heard about you.'

'And you made it your business?'

'Nope. I'd just finished with those three killers of my boss and I chanced to come this way and see you sitting there. It was pure luck. Bad luck for you, as it happens, good for me.'

'How many killers of your boss remain?'

The Growl would have counted on his fingers,

but his hand was a paw and sheathed in a glove, so he counted on his pointy teeth with his lolling tongue. It was a rapid calculation. 'Depends on how many there were to start with. Could be that just one is left alive.'

'Then your mission is almost over.'

'Not necessarily. There might be as many as four left. I will find out when I find out and not a second before.'

Ned nodded slowly and puffed out his cheeks.

'Why not go and get that pot?'

The Growl jerked his reins and cantered away, calling over his shoulder in a jocular voice, 'Coffee's coming.'

'I'll be right here when you get back,' said Ned, and he truly meant it. His eyes were full of prismatic tears.

But there was no fear in his heart.

Chapter Six
Monkey Man Manor

Russell was a small businessman with big ideas. He saw how cowboys loved to drink coffee and he wondered if they might also like to drink tea. He travelled in order to promote his trade and he took the utensils necessary for the preparation of a nice cup of tea with him. He called himself the 'tea mister' and that's how he introduced himself, but this was often misheard as *tea master* and he adopted the new designation without complaint. He was an easy-going man, Russell, all his impatience brewed to a standstill.

The problem was that he lacked good fortune, and although he strived hard his business never really flourished, and not much could be done about this. He was eventually reduced to venturing into the rougher lands of the far West, in a desperate attempt to sell sacks of tea. He rode up to a large ranch one morning in Tuolumne County and approached the overseer. 'I'm a tea mister,' were his first words. The overseer was pleased.

'A teamster, huh? Then we have need of you.'

'No, a tea mister.'

'That's what I said. A teamster. Shortage of good

teamsters round here. It seems to me you can start immediately. Pay is two dollars a day. That's pretty good wages for this part of the world.'

'I brew cups of tea.'

'Really don't care what you do in your spare time. Just glad to know there is a new teamster on the ranch. The stables are over there and wagons are next to the stables. Do what you know best and I'll meet you back here in one hour. Be real nice to see a wagon hitched.'

The hour passed and when the overseer returned, he was surprised to note that the best wagon on the ranch had been hitched to a giant teapot on very tiny wheels. Russell sat on the seat and the reins in his hands were looped around the lid of the teapot, which was steaming. The teapot had been stored in parts in his backpack and he'd assembled it rapidly. There were crankshafts and pistons too. It was a primitive steam engine.

'Cup of tea?' he asked.

'Dang! I only drink coffee,' said the overseer.

'Why don't you try it?'

'No way. I have tried too many new things in my life and it hasn't exactly worked out. Let me give you examples,' and he treated Russell to a condensed version of his life story. 'No tea for me,' he concluded, 'and if you aren't truly a teamster, there's no job here for you.'

Russell sadly drove off.

The teapot wasn't quite as efficient or strong as a horse, even though it was extremely modern, and it took him until nightfall to cross the ranch and roll up the slopes of the undulating hills that surrounded it. On the very top of one hill he found a copse of trees and entered it.

In the middle of the copse was a small glade and in the middle of the glade was a man. He was making camp. He sat around a fire with low flames and now Russell could see there was no coffee pot bubbling away. This fella didn't have one. He cleared his throat politely.

The figure looked up. It was wearing a cowl.

'Cup of tea?' said Russell.

There was a pause that lasted a full minute.

'Sure,' said The Growl.

Russell dismounted and placed a cup on the ground under the spout of the huge teapot. Then he wedged his shoulder under the handle of the pot, straining to lift it. The pot tilted and tea poured from the spout and filled the cup. Russell handed the cup to the stranger.

The Growl sipped it. 'That's welcome.'

'I'm a tea mister.'

The Growl nodded at this. He didn't mishear or ask any questions. He just lapped the tea with his tongue.

Russell decided to say nothing about the fact the man looked like a dog. It was none of his business anyway.

'My first time in Tuolumne County,' he said.

'Mine too,' said The Growl.

'Oh really? Where are you from originally, if you

don't mind me asking? I don't mean to be too nosy.'

'That's fine. I don't mind telling you. I was a newspaperman in St Louis, a fairly decent job, but now I'm–'

He left the sentence hanging and grinned.

'Hey!' said Russell.

'Anything wrong?' asked The Growl.

Russell answered:

'No, I'm just marvelling at a coincidence. Down there, on that ranch, is an overseer who was telling me about how once he was part of a vicious gang that murdered a newspaper editor in St Louis. He said that people kept telling him to try new things and killing a random fella seemed pretty new to him, so that is what he did. Put him off trying new things, though he had to learn new things when he became an overseer, but those new things were unavoidable. He hoped to avoid all other new things.'

The Growl was on his feet in an instant.

Russell backed away.

'Don't be frightened,' said The Growl.

'You are unhappy.'

'No, pard, I'm actually delighted. I have been searching for that fella for a long time. I have found him thanks to you. Wait here. I'm going down the hill. I will be back in due course. I wouldn't have known of a ranch over there if you hadn't told me. I'm obliged.'

'Don't tell him you sent me!' pleaded Russell.

'Won't tell him anything.'

GROWL AT THE MOON

The Growl vanished on foot through the trees. It was very dark now and as the embers of the fire winked out one by one, Russell shivered. He sat down and tried to relax. The Growl's horse eyed the giant teapot enviously, even though a stallion is much faster than a crude engine of that sort. But it is possible to envy crude things, Russell reasoned.

He felt sleepy now and his head nodded. Then he heard a stick break under a foot and he jerked back to full awareness. The Growl had returned. His frown was profound. He said, 'That was one of the killers, sure enough. He murdered my former boss, Ridley Smart.'

'What about the other killers?' asked Russell.

The Growl heaved a sigh.

'That's just it. I have no idea how many there are. He might have been the sixth and last but before I shot him I interrogated him. He told me that seven or eight took part in the attack. Maybe nine. He wasn't sure. But that means there's at least one left to hunt down.'

'And maybe as many as three, huh?'

The Growl nodded.

'I'll get them,' he said. He flapped his arms. 'Any chance of another cup of tea? I don't suppose you have any biscuits to dunk in it? No, well, that's not a surprise. Few biscuits out here.'

'Plenty of fugitives, though, I suppose?'

'Yes, unluckily.'

'Fugitives aren't much like biscuits. You can't dunk 'em. I mean, you can, if you wish, but it's no good.'

The Growl pondered this statement and then he nodded slowly. He nodded a lot, just as everyone else in the West did. They nodded in the daytime, nodded during the night, nodded in saloons and nodded while eating beans with spoons, nodded in a shootout, nodded when playing chess with showgirls, nodded when riding at full gallop, nodded if shopping for trollops, not that there was much to buy in the stores out here, only hats, huge hats that amplified the effect of a tiny nod and made it into a massive movement of the head on a neck. The Growl had a nod that was the best in the West.

'Can't dunk 'em,' he agreed, nodding again as he accepted the second cup of tea from the gratified tea mister.

Russell travelled with The Growl for many weeks, and although The Growl was a taciturn sort of companion, rarely saying more than forty-seven words in one day, he was pleasant enough. He was kind to animals, Russell noted, something that gladdened his heart. And he never criticised tea or wished it was coffee. The Growl was, in fact, a thoroughly good human being, except he wasn't fully human, but partly a good dog too.

'My dream,' Russell told him, 'is to grow tea everywhere, on the slopes of every range of hills, on terraces on the sides of every mountain, even in the lowlands, but I know that's a foolish idea. Tea doesn't like flat ground. It hates flat ground for some odd reason.'

'The odd reason is that it's too even?'

'Well said, wish I'd thought of that. I'm a tea mister but I'm no genius. At times I even wonder about that.'

'About what, pard?'

'Whether I'm a proper tea mister.'

'Huh? A tea miser?'

'Not a *miser*. A mister. A miser hoards stuff but a mister shares it. Could be interesting to speculate on what might happen if a miser collected misters. Would the miser be able to hoard them or would the misters share themselves until the miser was bereft of misters?'

'I just don't know.'

'But this philosophy's kinda fun, no?'

'That's right. No.'

They travelled slowly, because Russell's teapot wagon was only a quarter as speedy as The Growl's stallion.

But The Growl wasn't in a rush. He felt he would get all the killers of his boss and it didn't matter how long it took. It occurred to him that he ought to force one of them to explain *why* they had targeted Ridley Smart. He doubted that it truly was a random assault.

The world was a complex place, a maze on which a million games were being played simultaneously, and cheats outnumbered honest players and the umpires and referees were cheats too, or absent, and nobody knew the score, maybe there wasn't even a scoring system. His boss had been murdered in a restaurant and for dessert The Growl was going to eliminate every villain who had taken part in the foul crime.

Russell poured cups of tea for them both as they went along. The Growl mostly drank in silence and there was no conversation at all. He rarely or never asked for sugar or milk. Sometimes he would offer a few remarks when he was almost finished and there were only a dozen wet leaves at the bottom of his cup and these remarks were cryptic.

Very occasionally, The Growl became verbose.

He would twitch his snout.

'You remind me of a fella named Jorge. He was my companion for a short while and I kinda miss him. We had a duel and I didn't miss him then. But now I do. I have a hankering to visit his country. Argentina, it is called. And after I finish my quest for vengeance, I reckon I'll get down there, maybe even retire. He told me many things about it.'

'Do they drink tea in that land, did he mention?'

'Said nothing about that.'

'I won't risk it then. I'll retire somewhere else.'

'Really love tea, huh?'

'Like some men love women or horses.'

The Growl chuckled.

'Keeps you sane, I reckon. Or insane. Whichever you happen to be, but it keeps you that way, and that's a comfort. Could be whisky, tobacco or playing cards, but in your case, it's tea.'

'And in your case?'

'I don't have a case. I have a saddlebag.'

'What's inside it?'

'Symbolically, you mean? The saddlebag of my soul? Well, I love it when there's a full moon and it rises over the horizon and I am all alone in the middle of nowhere and I can growl.'

'Howl, you mean? You howl at the moon?'

'I do that too, yes, I howl. But that's not what I am talking about right now. I growl at the moon, a low note.'

Russell said after a spell, 'Each to his own.'

The Growl said, 'Yeah.'

It was a soft night when they had that conversation. They were riding east because there wasn't much west left before they hit the sea. It was random, this wandering of theirs, and as the days passed Russell started to feel affection for his dogfaced friend, as well as respect and admiration, but he was also puzzled by his behaviour. It wasn't just the fact he often acted like a hound but that he dropped hints about magic powers.

Russell decided to confront him openly on the topic one day. 'I am a man who takes pride in his grasp of logic. I am something of an engineer, in fact, as well as a business figure. Do you really believe there are forces in the universe that can't be explained by science?'

'I don't know about any of that. Maybe science *can* explain 'em. It's just that I don't think science has tried.'

'Do you have magic powers? That's the issue.'

'It isn't the issue, pard.'

The Growl sighed and turned in his saddle to face the little businessman on the seat of a wagon that was pulled by a giant teapot. 'My powers are limited. I am still a novice, that's why. But an experienced shaman can do wonderful feats of magnificence that are baffling. I know it for a fact. Others know it too, folks who are just like me, man-beasts.'

'There are other hybrids loose in the land?'

'Dozens of 'em, pard.'

'Are we likely to meet any?'

'It's not beyond the bounds of possibility.'

Russell shuddered.

He felt a delicious thrill fill the empty spaces of his psyche at the notion of encountering dog-men, cat-men and who knows what else? And only a few days later his wish was granted. They were passing through a barren valley in Utah, a blasted place forsaken not only by the gods but also by devils, when they found a delirious and dehydrated traveller who was lost. They revitalised him with tea and waited for him to fully recover.

Just like The Growl he wore a cowl, and when he removed it they saw that he was half badger, and he explained that his name was Doug, the pupil of one of the Mojave shamans, who had taken a wrong turn and ended up here. He had no horse and his boots were tattered.

'Ride on the wagon with me,' said Russell.
Doug accepted the offer.

Russell learned a lot by listening to the conversations that The Growl and Doug had as they travelled. Shamans were in place all over the land, but the best were in the Mojave Desert and they lived in caves. If you went into one of the caves and were trapped by a rockfall this meant that you were destined to become the latest pupil of that particular shaman.

The vast majority of shamans were half animal. A very few were half plant or half mineral but it was unclear whether these were genuine shamans who had gone wrong somewhere along the line or ordinary men in costumes. The Growl confessed to Doug that he wished the plural of shaman was *shamen* rather than the clumsier shamans, and Doug confessed the same thing right back at him. It helped the two men-beasts to bond.

Doug told The Growl about the Monkey Man. The Growl had heard a few rumours but didn't know much. He was said to be the fastest gun in the West, a capuchin monkey who didn't wear an artificial cowl because the markings of his fur made it seem he already had a cowl on. He lived in a treehouse somewhere, but it wasn't an ordinary treehouse.

'It's a manor! Absolutely huge with many rooms.'

'Built in a tree, you say?'

'The tree must be the largest and tallest tree in the world to bear the weight of such a stately home. Monkey Man lives alone but he doesn't need servants to keep the place clean because he prefers it dirty. He keeps an extensive collection of bananas in the highest chamber.'

'Some kind of simian aesthete, is he?'

'I reckon,' said Doug.

'Maybe even a *fin de siècle* decadent?'

'I dunno about that.'

It turned out that the badger-man didn't know the meaning of *fin de siècle*, in fact he didn't know any French at all and The Growl had to explain, 'It's the time period we associate with the turn of the century. Decadence is fashionable. Connoisseurs simper and prance.'

'The turn of the century? The late 1700s?'

'No, the next century.'

'But that's in the future!' objected Doug.

'Precisely. I am saying that Monkey Man is futuristic. He's a *fin de siècle* fella, in other words he acts in ways that no one else does, or will do for another few years. He is ahead of himself.'

'His head is certainly very hairy,' said Doug, 'but I don't know if it's truly of himself. I suppose it might be.'

'Indubitably, pard,' commented The Growl.

Russell now muttered:

'I don't understand half of what you two are saying, and of the half that I do understand I only comprehend about one quarter, but it's mighty interesting all the same. Glad I met you!'

'Well, there are things about you that *we* don't understand, so it seems we are equal,' observed The Growl.

'What things?' wondered Russell.

'How come your weird teapot chariot keeps on the boil even though there is no wood or coal in the furnace.'

'I was mighty curious about that too,' said Doug.

'Seems supernatural,' said The Growl.

'Miraculous,' added Doug.

Russell laughed and soothed the mild apprehension of the dog-man and the badger-man by explaining the workings of his vehicle. They understood about the cogs and gears and axles and crankshafts, but they were uncertain about the power source. Russell continued:

'It is powered by strange stones that I found one day, here in Utah, in fact, about ten miles south of the town of Blandings. They glowed in the dark. Then I saw that they radiated heat. I collected sackfuls of them and ground them down into a powder and put the powder in a jar. I breathed some of the dust in and my lungs burned for weeks. They still ache a little. Anyway, the jar is positioned at the base of the teapot chariot.'

'And it keeps the water boiling without flames?'

'Yup, it's a scientific marvel.'

'Do you think that powder might be dangerous?'

Russell shook his head.

'Nah,' he said. 'Some of my skin flaked off and my hair fell out shortly after I discovered the rocks, but that was coincidence. Anyway I feel fine now, just dizzy once in a while.'

'Dizzy is nothing to worry about,' opined Doug. 'I get dizzy myself each time I play chess with a showgirl.'

'Funny how playing chess with showgirls has become acceptable in just the past few weeks,' said Russell.

'Not so long ago it was considered very peculiar,' said The Growl, and he thought wistfully of his friend Jorge, who had enjoyed the activity before others had learned to appreciate it.

Doug rubbed his snout and said:

'It happens. The same way that making duck noises is a craze. They come and go, these fads. But playing chess with showgirls is more than a fad. I think it could become a tradition.'

The Growl looked at him thoughtfully. 'Do you play the *en passant* rule? I am just curious about that.'

Doug shook his head. 'I don't speak French.'

'It's a nice language.'

'But what's the use of it in the States?'

'Ever been in Louisiana?'

'One day I might go there, just for the music, but I'm in no rush. I knew a fella once by the name of Geddy. He was always in a rush. But that's beside the point. I'm happy just speaking English and Spanish and a little bit of Navajo. It seems to me that actions speak louder than any language, even though "actions" is a word that can be translated.'

'*Plus fort que les mots,*' agreed The Growl.

'Maybe,' laughed Doug.

'Anyway, I am wondering about Monkey Man and his manor. I'd like to see it with my own eyes one day.'

'That mightn't be wise. What if it angers him?'

'Perhaps it will. Too bad.'

'A tree house in the tallest tree, my friend.'

'Must be a redwood.'

'I was thinking along the same lines.'

'You think along lines? Me too. I have thought along lines ever since I saw my first train go past. It was on the horizon and the flaring smokestack belched thick black clouds into a sky tortured by the flying cinders that escaped from the firebox and I was enchanted.'

'Enchanted, sure. Engrossed too?'

'A little bit of engrossment, but enchantment mostly.'

Russell interrupted now:

'Is that the correct usage of the word "engrossment". I thought it meant the final version of a legal document?'

'Maybe so,' admitted The Growl. He winked.

Doug said dispassionately:

'The lines I think along aren't straight like a railway. They are curves and loops. Tie themselves in knots often. If you try to cut them, they'll entangle the blade you're using, metaphorically.'

'I don't think in lines at all,' said Russell.

'Really?' said The Growl.

'My thought patterns are blobs of abstract colour. They swirl like tea. That is just the way I am made.'

'Does that mean you are an artistic soul?'

'Could be,' said Russell.

'The sort of man who thinks that clouds make shapes because they want to entertain people on the ground?'

'Spot on,' said Russell.

'One more thing,' said The Growl.

'Sure,' said Russell.

'How did you manage to fit the disassembled parts of the giant teapot *and* all the sacks of tea in one backpack?'

'Compression,' answered Russell proudly.

The Growl laughed.

Between them, the trio worked out that Monkey Man's manor was probably to be found in Northern California or Southern Oregon, where the redwoods grow tallest, and The Growl said:

'I been to California so many times that I want to give it a break. But I'm happy to travel to Oregon.'

'Let's go there then,' said Doug.

Russell said, 'We are facing the wrong way and it's quite difficult for me to turn my teapot chariot around. Why don't we go to Oregon some other time and keep going this way for now?'

'Can't you put that thing into reverse?'

'Not easily,' admitted Russell. 'It runs forwards on tea, you see, and if I wanted to make it go in the other direction I'd have to run it on the opposite of tea. The problems are considerable.'

'What is the opposite of tea? Coffee?'

'No, coffee is a *rival* to tea, but it ain't the opposite. I don't actually know what the opposite of tea is. That's the difficulty. It's not biscuits. I don't think it is rum or beer. Could be gravel.'

'Forget it then,' said Doug.

The Growl squinted at the sun. It was noon.

'We have been drifting a little south even though we are heading east. We will be back in Mexico soon.'

Russell almost shouted:

'*Back* in Mexico? I never went there.'

'Well, if you'd really like to visit it, I don't mind. We can go there just to take a look around. I'm easy.'

They both looked at the badger-man.

Doug shrugged.

He mumbled, 'If my name wasn't Doug, I wouldn't shrug. If it was Rod, I would nod, and if it was Fred I'd go to bed.' He spoke more loudly, 'Mexico is fine by me. They got tequila.'

He licked his lips and smiled. The others nodded and so they continued to trundle along over the rutted road.

'I *am* Doug,' said the badger-man firmly.

'You bet,' said Russell.

They saw in the distance an object that looked

like a booth. As they neared it, they realised that it really *was* a booth. An upright wooden box like a coffin in which stood a man. There was a counter before him and on the counter stood a big earthen vessel with a tap set into its base. He was watching them with eyes that were jubilant but desperate.

'Howdy, strangers. Thirsty work, riding?'

'Reckon so,' said Doug.

'May I interest you in some refreshing juice?'

'Dunno. What kind is it?'

'Cactus juice,' said the booth-keeper.

The Growl frowned. 'Cactus juice? Tequila, you mean?'

The booth-keeper smiled.

'Nope. Just the juice. You drink it then you gotta hold it in your stomach until it ferments. That's the only way you'll get drunk on it. Don't empty your bladder for a couple of days.'

'You squeeze it out of cactuses around here?'

'Plural of *cactus* is cacti.'

'Cactuses is also correct. It depends on the dictionary. I don't use either myself, though,' said The Growl.

'What *do* you use?'

'I don't. I ignore the prickly little varmints.'

'But the juice is tasty!'

'Maybe so,' conceded The Growl. He peered more closely at the man and frowned. 'Do I know you?'

'Never met before. No siree.'

'Now about this cactus juice of yours –'

The booth-keeper was plainly agitated. He said, 'I got a private source for my juice. Why not sample some?'

'I'm easy,' said Doug.

'I'm difficult,' said The Growl. Then he softened. 'But I'll try your juice anyway. See no harm in it.'

The booth-keeper filled three clay cups from the earthen vessel. As he did so, his body jerked up and down. He was standing on something and trampling it for some reason. Was he extracting juice from cacti while his customers were watching him prepare the drinks?

His legs were hidden by the base of the solid counter. He certainly wasn't alone in that booth. A series of muffled groans came from behind the counter. Do cacti groan when they are hurt?

'What you got down there?' asked The Growl.

'Nothing, my friend.'

'You are trampling something.'

'Just drink your juice and enjoy it. Questions are unnecessary here. I do what I gotta do to earn a living.'

Russell and Doug had already drunk half a cup each of the juice, but The Growl left his untouched and said:

'I demand to see what's inside with you.'

The booth-keeper's nostrils flared. He stared hard at The Growl and then he grinned. He whipped out a shotgun from some recess but despite his speed he was far too slow to triumph over the cowled dog-man. The gun was in the gloved hand of The Growl in the blink of a fly's eye and a shot rang out. Then the booth-keeper sagged and leaked.

The Growl peered over the edge of the counter.

'There's a man there!'

'What do you mean?' cried Doug.

'He's been trampling on a man, a badly injured fella. The juice has been coming out of his wounds.'

Russell and Doug exchanged disgusted looks.

'Liquid cannibalism, huh?'

'Not exactly,' said The Growl. 'He's not entirely human. He's part plant. In fact, he's a cactus-man.'

'The same way you're a dog-man and Doug here is a badger-man? I guess he studied with a shaman too?'

'He *is* a shaman,' concluded The Growl, and he added, 'People who study with the Mojave wizards will turn partly into animals, but never into plants. It's simply not possible. But a tiny minority of shamans are partly plant themselves. It's very unusual to see one.'

'We are privileged,' explained Doug.

Russell absorbed this.

'Privileged but disturbed,' he cried.

'Yup,' said Doug.

The Growl put their minds at ease.

'The juice you two fellas have just drunk was only partly blood, so don't feel too bad. Feel just the right amount of guilt, no more, OK? The rest of that liquid was genuine cactus juice.'

'Well, that's half a relief,' said Russell.

Doug said sadly, 'True enough, but it looks like the booth-keeper gave no *quarter* to the poor cactus dude.'

'No quarter? He didn't even spare him a dime!'

'A dime? That's novel.'

The Growl reached forward and pulled the booth-keeper over the counter and dumped him on the ground.

'He is still alive. I want to question him. I feel I vaguely recognise him. I am sure we have never met before, which means it's my doggy senses that are alerting me to something strange.'

The Growl kneeled by the booth-keeper's side.

'Hey,' he said, as his nose twitched. 'I reckon this fella is one of the guys who killed my boss, Ridley Smart.'

'Can you be absolutely certain?' asked Russell.

'No, but he smells like –'

The booth-keeper stirred and blood trickled out of his mouth. His speech was slurred but intelligible. 'Yeah, that's right. I was one of his killers. I'd heard there was a vigilante picking us off one by one. That's you, huh? A meeting was inevitable, I guess. The gang split up, mostly, and I came here to try to make an openly dishonest buck selling the ichor of a rare shaman. Never made much but we do what we can to stay alive.'

'You're not staying alive now,' said The Growl.

'Good point, crisply made.'

'My doggy senses are pretty reliable, but it's the hard way of doing things. I prefer easier ways. I want you to tell me how many members of the gang there were and where the others are?'

'Ten is the answer.'

'I was told nine was the maximum.'

'Then someone lied to you. That's not uncommon. People lie all the time. They say they are rich when they ain't. They say they can do duck impressions when they can't. They say they can balance on stilts but it turns out they'll fall off almost instantly if they try.'

'Are you certain?'

'About ducks and stilts?'

'No, the gang.'

'Ten members in total. I was the only one who took care to count them. I was under the impression that some of us were professional killers while others were strictly amateur. I was one of the amateurs. How many you killed so far? I estimate it at six, is that correct?'

'Seven including you,' said The Growl.

'Three to go then.'

'Now tell me where they can be found?'

'I dunno about two of them. We split up, like I said, and lost contact with each other. The third one, fella named Cooper, went down to Mexico. He said he was going to dig for treasure.'

'Mexico is a big place. Where exactly?'

'Somewhere in the Sierra Madre Mountains. That's all I know. Never been there myself, so can't pinpoint anything with any accuracy. Look. I am dying. I deserve to be left in peace.'

'Left in pieces? Sure, I can do that.'

'Please! It's over.'

Doug stepped up and rested his hand on The Growl's shoulder. 'Vengeance should be clean and pure, never messy. Don't torture him. He has given you the information you asked for. What about the cactus shaman? Can he be saved? He is more important right now.'

The Growl accepted this. He stood and turned away from the booth-keeper but as a final blow he never even asked the killer's name. He would die here, an unburied corpse, a birthday present for some vulture or other and his name was of no interest to anyone or anything. The Growl returned to the booth and with a growl he seized it and ripped it apart.

The body of the trampled cactus shaman was exposed. Russell hastened to fetch a cup of medicinal tea for him.

'Reckon he's in no condition to sip anything,' said The Growl. Reverently he removed his cowl and showed the dying shaman his elongated face. 'I was a pupil,' he said. 'I studied with Tony.'

'Tony?' gasped the cactus shaman. 'I remember him well. We were great pals when we were young. Is he?'

'No, he's not dead. Well, not exactly.'

'Your words are mysterious, my son. But I thank you for liberating me. It was horrible being squeezed all day.'

'I bet! I know that being squeezed is sometimes

agreeable, like when you lose a game of chess and a showgirl squeezes you because that was the bet, but I can't think of other good squeezes.'

'My name is Fred,' croaked the cactus shaman.

'Honoured to meet you.'

'Yeah, they all say that. But in your case, I believe it.' He chuckled and a green froth bubbled down his chin.

And Fred the cactus closed his eyes forever.

'Better not wrap him in a shroud. His prickles will punch holes in it, plus we don't have one spare,' said Doug.

'We'll cremate him instead, using the wood of the booth as a pyre. That's the most dignified ending,' said The Growl, and he began gathering armfuls of the splintered booth and piling them.

The others helped. The funeral was held just after sunset. They didn't care to camp in the vicinity, so they resumed travelling. They had two destinations now and both were viable. The Sierra Madre Mountains to seek out and kill the killer known as Cooper. And then back and onwards to Oregon to find Monkey Man and his remarkable tree house.

Crossing back into Mexico presented no serious challenges. They thought of themselves as 'the three amigos', not because it was a profound thing to think, but because it *wasn't*. It's nice to relax your brain once in a while. In the desert they had one of those unexpected but useful encounters that made them wonder how real the world was. It was too convenient.

They came upon an abandoned locomotive, lying on its side next to a set of disused rails. Russell examined it and declared the engine to be serviceable. The train was in perfectly good condition. The railway tracks were fine too. It must have been abandoned for economic or political rather than technical reasons. It was rusty, true, but not damaged.

If only it were possible to lift the locomotive engine back onto the tracks! Then they could pour tea into the boiler and Russell's burning ore dust in a jar would power it. The train would take them down through Mexico in style and far more efficiently than the teapot chariot could. Even The Growl's horse was slow in comparison. They pondered.

Infrequently, they stopped pondering to mull instead, and sometimes they even ceased mulling in order to contemplate. But eventually they came back to the act of pondering and finally The Growl said, in a low voice that was anxious and proud at the same time, 'Yes.'

'Huh? Yes what?'

'Yes, I think I can lift it.'

'Are you joking? The tonnage is enormous!'

'Not with my muscles, I don't mean that, but with magic. Yeah, I think I know a spell to do the trick.'

Russell said, 'You told me that your magical

powers were very limited and the drain on your energy levels is excessive. What if you injure yourself in the process? It's too risky.'

'Pard, the only truly risky thing in life is never taking risks,' and despite his habitual modesty, The Growl was pleased with himself for inventing such a memorable maxim on the spur of the moment. The spur of the moment showed him at his best only occasionally. He preferred the stirrup of the moment, saddle of the moment, even the reins of the moment. Then he dismounted, approached the locomotive and said slowly:

'I can turn myself into a pack of dogs.'

'A pack of dogs!'

'That's what I said. I've never done it before, so it's all theoretical, but I'm sure I can manage it. One dog ain't enough to set a toppled train upright, but an entire pack of 'em might do it.'

'I can't turn myself into lots of badgers,' said Doug.

'That's a pity,' said Russell.

'It's going to require a tremendous effort and you are going to have to look after me for many days afterwards, maybe a week or so, nursing me, giving me cups of tea regularly. Is that OK?'

'Don't see why not,' answered Russell.

Doug also nodded.

'Pack of dogs, here I come!'

Russell turned to Doug, 'A *pack* of dogs, he said?' He puffed his cheeks, a faraway look in his eyes. 'Wow.'

'Bow,' said Doug.

'Huh? I beg your pardon?'

'You said wow but dogs say bow. I was just correcting your syntax. Don't mind me, though. I'm easy.'

'Actually, they say bow *and* wow.'

Doug accepted this.

The Growl was preparing himself for the ritual. It would take an hour if he got it right, he warned them, six hours if he made any errors in the chanting and mind concentration exercises.

They didn't dare disturb him when he sat on the ground with crossed legs, closed his eyes, and made a low humming noise with his lips. Doug knew about this shaman stuff but Russell was fascinated by the novelty of it. He watched as The Growl descended or ascended, for he wasn't sure which, into another realm of being, a dimension of contemplation and mind expansion and all sorts of odd mentalist shenanigans. He said:

'Wish I had trained with a shaman.'

'It's not too late,' said Doug, 'but have you ever thought about what kind of animal you would like to be?'

'Yes, I have, but I won't tell you now.'

'I'll ask again in the future. Don't want to harass your sense of privacy. It is good to keep some secrets.'

Russell nodded. He waited with Doug as The Growl mumbled a complex chant that went on for a long time. It rose and fell in volume and the music of it was extremely strange, with lots of quarter notes and intricate rhythms. At times it sounded like a madman forcing a squeaky shoe through the reinforced strings of a strange banjo. At other times it was like birds singing about the benefits of wildflower honey. The time passed.

It took two and a half hours before the spell was cast. Abruptly The Growl vanished in a puff of blue smoke. The smoke quickly dissipated. Smoke always leads a dissipated life, Doug noted.

They were expecting a pack of dogs to be standing where The Growl had been sitting, a large pack of very large hounds capable of pushing a locomotive back onto the railway tracks, but instead rectangular objects floated down. They landed on the ground very gently.

Doug stepped closer and frowned.

He said, 'Playing cards.'

'How many?'

'A whole *pack* of 'em.'

'Are they normal playing cards? Pick them up.'

Doug did so. He looked at them and shook his head. All the suits showed a different breed of dog. The royal cards displayed dogs dressed like monarchs. It was a pack of dogs, certainly, but not at all the kind they had been waiting for. It was no help whatsoever. The Growl had clearly messed up the spell or else his magic simply wasn't good enough.

'What shall we do now?' asked Russell.

Doug licked his lips.

'Play with them, I guess, and hope he changes back.'

'Will the spell wear off?'

'I hope so, sonny, otherwise we have lost him forever. And he's the best of us. Shall we play a game of poker?'

'I don't know the rules. Can we play cribbage?'

'Sure, I prefer that.'

They squatted and played cribbage and kept score by writing the numbers in the earth. They played for half an hour and then the cards vanished and The Growl sat there in a daze, blinking and clutching his sore head. He said, 'Sorry but I couldn't quite manage it.'

'But it was a difficult spell,' soothed Doug.

'I overestimated myself.'

'It happens, in fact it's common, even natural. We played cribbage and that was worthwhile. But what next?'

'We'll have to forget about the train.'

Russell now spoke up:

'I'm not sure about that. I have an idea. Why don't we try to use my teapot chariot to push the locomotive? At full power I believe it might be just powerful enough to attain the objective.'

The Growl frowned. 'I do love an attained objective. But is the ore dust in the jar fierce enough to heat up the tea sufficiently to create enough pressure in the pot to propel the wheels with sufficient force to enable the chariot to budge the train along? I have my doubts.'

'The ore dust isn't fierce enough right now, but I can agitate it by stirring it and then it will be furious.'

'Isn't that dangerous?' ventured Doug.

'Yes, if I stir it with a stick, the stick might catch fire. So I had better use my bare hands. Mind you, the powder might burn my hands, so I ought to test it on my eyes first. I think that's best.'

'What if it burns your eyes?' cried The Growl.

'You're right. I hadn't thought of that,' admitted Russell. 'I'd better test it on my manroot first, to be sure.'

'You need seclusion to do that?' asked Doug.

'Nobody is around here to see. And I count you as friends. I don't suppose it will offend you? So let's do it.'

He walked towards the giant teapot and opened a hatch in the base. He put his hand inside the hatch and pulled out a large jar. The dust inside glowed and it audibly crackled. The Growl and Doug watched as Russell unscrewed the lid, dropped his trousers and gently lowered his manroot into the powder. His face scrunched up and his lips were tightly compressed, but a whimper of pain came out of them nonetheless. He said:

'Yes, it has burned my tooter. Which means it will probably sting my eyes, so let's make sure, eh?' And he flung a pinch of powder into his face. He yelled and staggered around, blinking, the tears streaming down his cheeks. His vision was blurred, for he knocked into The Growl and rebounded and struck Doug. It was several minutes before he said:

'Damn, that hurts! It means that it's strong enough to sting my eyes, which means it will probably damage my hands too. Like this.' And he plunged with a scream both arms deep into the jar.

'Stirring it around, are you?' questioned Doug.

'Yes, I goddam am!'

He pulled out his arms, screwed the lid back on the jar, returned the jar to the alcove in the teapot, closed the hatch, mounted the wagon, pulled the reins and released the brake. He shouted:

'Let's see what this teatime beauty can do!'

He trundled forwards.

The teapot chariot connected with the bulk of the locomotive engine and it ground to a halt, but the wheels kept turning, digging runnels in the ground. The whine of metal turned into a squeal.

'Maximum torque!' yelled Russell. 'Tea squared multiplied by dust to the power of powder. Dead ahead.'

'Dead's an unlucky word, pard,' said The Growl.

'Onward teapot soldiers!'

Slowly, very slowly, the locomotive began to shift, and once it had started moving the motion accelerated.

But at the same time, the giant teapot gradually crumpled under the strain. A race was on. Which would succumb first? The train or the chariot? Russell's expression was ecstatic. He felt he was going to win. The Growl and Doug now clapped encouragement. Maybe they used their limited magical powers to help the chariot. Who knows? They probably didn't even know themselves, for much magic is performed subconsciously.

The teapot had been compressed to half its size. Steam leaked from gaps in the twisted panels and the spout spat scalding tea in huge globs of flavour. The Growl worried that the whole thing would explode. His gun was in his hand in a blink and he prepared to open up safety vents in the side of the teapot with his bullets if it should become necessary.

But there was no need for that. With a great groaning and a pinging of old springs, like a chorus of showgirls bouncing on an antique bed, the locomotive was pushed onto the rails. It rocked upright and for an instant it seemed it had been pushed too hard and would topple over on its other side. But no, it came back down and settled into position.

The giant teapot was mangled beyond recognition.

'Hey, what's that?' cried Doug.

'Dunno,' said The Growl.

'It's the teapot. It's mangled beyond recognition. That's why you're unable to recognise it,' explained Russell.

'Oh yes. Well, you've done a good job there.'

'We have our own train.'

'Better fill it up with water and tea leaves and then transfer the jar of dust to the firebox in the crew compartment. Let's hope the rails go as far as we are planning to travel and don't just suddenly come to an abrupt end after a couple of miles. The Sierra Madre Mountains!'

Russell said, 'There's something I've been meaning to say.' He blushed a little and looked at the ground.

'What is it, pard? You can tell us anything.'

'Well, it's just this,' said Russell. 'You both keep referring to them as the Sierra Madre Mountains. But 'Sierra' means 'Mountains', so you are doubling a word and that's a waste of energy.'

The Growl nodded. 'Glad you told us, pard.'

'You aren't annoyed?'

'Not at all. I ain't no young pup to get offended when someone points out my errors. I respect you for it.'

'Me too,' said Doug. Russell was relieved.

'Let's fix her up.'

They filled the boiler, salvaged the jar from the teapot and placed it in the locomotive's firebox. Then The Growl cried, 'All aboard,' and he smiled as he added, 'for the Sierra Madre!'

'Bon voyage to us,' called Doug.

They were off. The track kept going and although it was in bad condition in a few places, they were able to proceed. The route avoided most urban centres. It passed through a dozen ghost towns and they saw very few people. At last they came to a place where the rails ran straight into the side of a cliff and The

Growl applied the brakes. They ground to a halt just a few inches short of a collision. It was the end of the line. They got out.

'Mighty funny terminus to a railway line.'

'They probably planned to drill a tunnel through the cliff but never started the job,' commented The Growl.

Doug and Russell inspected their surroundings.

'A mountain range.'

'The Sierra Madre, I suppose?'

'Must be,' said Doug. 'The fella you are searching for is here somewhere and he is searching for treasure.'

'I will be the treasure he finds,' said The Growl.

'Almost feel sorry for him.'

'Me too. But hey, that's the way things happen to be. The world is a tough place and my heart is tougher.'

'Nah, there's a soft streak in you.'

The Growl acknowledged this with a small smile. 'Reckon you're right. It ain't like I was born to this kind of existence. I was Bill Bones, newspaperman, a city slicker for a long time. I had to learn outback life the hard way. I recall the first time I made water against a cactus and ended up with a savage prickle in my tickler. A valuable lesson.'

'My own tickler has turned green,' said Russell.

'Because of the dust?'

'Yeah, that powder is mighty curious stuff. But green is a healthy colour, ain't it? Like grass and leaves.'

'Guess so,' said The Growl, but in actual fact he hadn't taken a guess. He gazed at the mountains and noticed a path that led through them. He pointed it out. The three of them set off on foot.

They toiled upwards for several hours and then the path levelled and it was a joy to be up there, looking down on hidden valleys on both sides, halfway to the lowest clouds and the eagles. Now the path spiralled down and they entered a space that was hemmed in on all sides by sheer cliffs. It was a garden of wild fruit trees, a paradise among the rocks.

The man named Cooper was digging in the centre of the space, wiping his brow every now and then with a cloth. He looked up, frowned at the strangers. It wasn't that he recognised The Growl, simply that he resented intruders while he was in the act of digging for treasure.

'Just who the hell are you?' he demanded.

'Lucky fellas,' said The Growl.

'Really? Are you so sure you're lucky? Look at this! It's a gun and now I am going to shoot all three of you.'

'I am absolutely certain I am lucky,' answered The Growl, 'because I am on your trail and never expected to find you so easily. It might have taken weeks of sniffing around to locate you.'

Cooper had already fired but The Growl was ready for anything. He pulled the trigger and his own bullet met the enemy bullet in midair and because it was more powerful, coming from a larger calibre piece, it pushed Cooper's bullet in a reverse direction. Both bullets struck him but with much reduced force. They drew blood but penetrated no vital organ.

'Darn you!' he yelled.

'I am packing a Colt Walker with a .44 calibre and it's the most powerful handgun in the Old West so far. You are packing a .36-calibre Colt 1851 Navy revolver, a fine gun but no match for mine. I needed a more powerful gun and I bought one in San Antonio when I was there. But I'm not here to get technical. I am here to avenge my former boss.'

'Who the hell was he?'

'Ridley Smart, my editor back in St Louis.'

'Bah! I hate that city.'

The Growl wasted no more time on the scoundrel. He shot him dead and when Doug protested by saying, 'You never asked him where the other two fellas you are hunting can be found,' The Growl replied along the lines that he sensed Cooper didn't know and it didn't matter anyway, he would find them one day, and now it was time to leave Mexico and head back to Oregon and search for Monkey Man and his insane house.

Russell stroked his chin and asked quietly, 'What about the treasure he was digging for? Shall we dig too?'

'I don't believe in it,' said The Growl.

'Why not?' asked Doug.

The Growl twitched his nose and said, 'It don't smell right to me, pard. It smells like rancid old custard.'

'You think someone buried custard there?'

'I said it was *like* custard, not that it actually *is* custard. It's probably just a pair of crusty old pants. Whatever it is, it ain't gold, silver or gems. It ain't even tequila or rum. Believe me, pard.'

They trusted his doggy instincts. Lots of rumoured treasure turns out to be illusory and so they headed slowly back along the path to the spot where they had abandoned the train, but an unpleasant surprise waited for them there. The Mexican Captain who was standing next to his horse was just one of a troop of them, all dressed in dusty uniforms.

'We listen out for the echo of shots in the mountains, *señor*, and when we hear them we come here,' he said.

'To accept bribes, I imagine?' growled The Growl.

'No, *señor*. To keep the peace.'

'To keep it all for yourself, no doubt.'

The Captain frowned.

'I don't like your manners, *señor*, and I am going to ask you to decline to offer any resistance when I tell you that you're under arrest. Your *amigos* too. I am astonished, *señor*, by the sight of the three of you. A dog, a badger and one who is just very ugly. This is a serious matter. It can't be resolved with a bribe. I am going to march you to the jail.'

'Yes, I am a dog. You would do well to be a dog too. Yes, this fella here is a badger. It is always good to be friends with a badger. It's a shame you don't have any badgers among your men.'

'Badgers? We don't need no stinking badgers!'

'Do badgers stink?'

It was Russell who asked that.

The Growl bent close and sniffed Doug's fur. 'A bit,' he said. 'But that's not important. I refuse to be arrested. I also decline on your behalf. None of us are going to jail with this Captain.'

'Then I have no choice, *señor*, but to order my –'

He never finished his speech.

The Growl fired five shots and five men fell. Not because they had been hit but because the bullets had startled the horses, just as the dog-man had planned, and the horses had bolted and knocked down the men. The men were unhurt but just a bit dazed. The Growl shouted:

'Now's our chance!'

The Growl, Doug and Russell ran in the same direction as the horses. Ten minutes later they caught up with the steeds, which had slowed down, and they jumped into their saddles and applied their heels to the beasts' flanks and were riding hell for leather and heaven for wild flowers in a northerly direction, away from the Mountains and the Law.

One month later they were in Oregon. They trotted over the landscape and all was well, but Russell had been feeling sick. He was running a fever, his body often trembled and his ears were coming loose. He wondered what could be a likely reason for the symptoms. Probably all the beans they ate every evening for supper. Then his ears fell into his coffee mug and he concluded that yes, it was beans that were responsible.

Apart from that, everything was fine.

They reached the most heavily forested part of the state and they weaved a tortuous way through the mighty redwood trunks. They met very few people in this region and when they asked for directions to Monkey Man Manor, no one was able to tell them. Even a sasquatch shrugged his shoulders to indicate that he couldn't be of much help. So they kept going, aware that random wandering is often as good as targeted travel.

And poor Russell pined for tea, but The Growl said, 'Ain't no use *pining* for anything in a *redwood* forest.'

His words were always intended to be comforting.

But they very rarely were.

Doug was ahead of the other two. He sniffed the air and said, 'I'm not an expert of what monkeys smell like, but I just caught the hint of a twinge of the whiff of something a bit simian.'

'Any local monkey species in these parts?' asked Russell, and he was told that no, they weren't indigenous to Oregon, at least not now. Maybe thousands of years ago they had lived here.

Doug enjoyed displaying his knowledge. He had

read encyclopaedias when young and he was almost as well-read as The Growl. He had memorised many facts from the pages of the tomes.

'Some types of beasts never take root in certain continents. I never heard of pandas in Europe, for example.'

Russell came to a logical conclusion. 'That means that if you have smelled a monkey just now, there must be a monkey not too far away, and if monkeys do not live in Oregon as a species –'

'Then Monkey Man is near at hand.'

'I can't smell any monkey scent. All I can smell is bananas,' said Russell, disappointed with his nostrils.

'The odour of bananas is *concealing* the monkey aroma,' said Doug. The Growl nodded at this. 'You have to nose around under the banana smell to get to the other smell. Bananas aren't indigenous to Oregon, as far as I'm aware. I definitely think *he* is in the vicinity.'

They exchanged glances.

Then they decided they preferred the glances they had started with, so they took them back. 'Be alert,' they advised each other. They looked up in the high treetops for evidence of a house.

'His treehouse is said to be a manor, so it won't be easy to miss. I wonder how he managed to build it?'

'Did he employ workers?' asked Russell.

'I doubt it. His security relies on secrecy as much as his fabled quick-draw and how can you employ a team of labourers and then expect every one of them to keep their lips buttoned? At least one of them would blab and the location of Monkey Man Manor would be common knowledge. I reckon he built it himself, which means he is a remarkable creature, with determination as well as strength and agility, and a keen brain.'

That was The Growl's judgement.

Doug cried out.

They had entered a small clearing. It wasn't a proper clearing because the size of it was negligible. But the gaps between the trees at this point were rather wider. In the centre of this pseudo-clearing stood the mightiest tree trunk that any of them had ever beheld.

It was so thick that a man running in circles around it wouldn't be faster than the second hand of a clock running around a clock face. The bark shone in the sunlight that penetrated the forest canopy. Around the base of the redwood were piled thousands of banana skins in varying states of decay. The ones near the bottom of the mound were black, the ones near the top bright yellow, and a stench of bananas filled the fake glade. The eyes of the trio travelled up the full length of the towering trunk.

At the top was a house, a massive dwelling, so large that this particular tree only supported its main weight, for it straddled adjacent trees too. The design of the building was unusual and yet familiar. The Growl frowned at it and whistled until his neck ached from straining.

'It's a paddle steamer.'

'What do you mean?' cried Russell.

'My meaning is in the words I uttered. That house is a Mississippi paddle steamer. I can see the paddlewheels. Monkey Man is cleverer than I thought! He didn't construct a house up there.'

'What did he do?'

'He dragged a paddle steamer overland and hoisted it to the top of this tree and he lives on the ship. The ship *is* the treehouse. But dragging it all the way! It must have cost him a tremendous amount of effort. And then ropes and pulleys in order to raise it into position!'

'I feel like letting loose an oath,' confessed Doug.

'Then do so,' said The Growl.

'You misunderstand me. Not any old oath, such as what you might hear in a saloon, but an oath newly-coined right now, a meaningless word that I can call out for obscure cathartic reasons.'

'That's fine by me. Go right ahead.'

'Are you certain?'

The Growl and Russell nodded and Doug shouted, 'Fitzcarraldo!' and then he waited for the echoes to fade.

There was a pause and then they fell silent. The stench of the bananas was so thick it drifted like a mist around the tree. They heard a movement above, the branches groaned and leaves rustled. An object was travelling towards them at a remarkable speed, swinging down from branch to branch. It was Monkey Man himself and the grin on his face shone with a great intensity even at this range. The Growl waited patiently, Doug with mild agitation, Russell with a mixture of fear and fascination. Who knew how Monkey Man would respond to their visit to his abode? He might be angry.

Monkey Man stopped in the lowest branch, which was just above them. He wore no clothes but there was a belt around his waist and two holsters dangled from it, and in the holsters were two ripe bananas. On his back he carried some sort of pack on straps, a papoose in fact, and inside the papoose was a man who saluted them in a friendly fashion.

'I recognise that fellow!' cried The Growl.

'Who is he?' asked Doug.

But the man in the papoose answered in a booming voice, 'My name is Hardy and I met the gentleman in the cowl down there in Punta Arena a while ago. I was working on a project that went wrong. After it was over, I made my way here and gained employment.'

'What kind of job do you do?' asked Doug.

'I am an interpreter.'

'An interpreter for Monkey Man?'

'That's correct.'

The Growl frowned. 'May I speak with your boss?'

Hardy said, 'Of course.'

'He doesn't speak English at all?'

'Very little, just a few words. It would be better if you spoke Dog to him and he can answer in

Monkey.'

'I don't understand why,' said The Growl.

'It's perfectly straightforward,' explained Hardy. 'Communication is only possible, or rather it is *optimal*, when the language skills of both participants in a conversation approach equality. If the skills are perfectly equal, then that's the best situation for a conversation.'

'That doesn't really enlighten me on the topic.'

Hardy rolled his eyes.

'Yes, it does. Listen carefully. You are fluent in Dog but speak no Monkey. He is fluent in Monkey but speaks no Dog. Your language skills in this manner are identical, in the sense that you are absolutely unfluent in Monkey and he is absolutely unfluent in Dog. You are equally matched! We have already agreed that being equally matched is the key to perfect understanding. But if you spoke in English to each other, misunderstandings would be inevitable, for you would both be speaking a language in which there was a wide discrepancy in fluency. Speak Dog and he will speak Monkey and I will interpret and there will be no problems whatsoever, I promise.'

The Growl was bowled over by this and he could think of no objections to Hardy's explanation. He gazed up at Monkey Man and their eyes locked. With a small cough, The Growl cleared his throat. Then he ventured, 'Woof?' and then repeated the question louder, 'Woof?'

'Oo,' said Monkey Man.

'Woof? Woof!' inquired The Growl.

'Oo,' Monkey Man said.

'Woof! Woof woof? Woof woof!'

'Oo oo oo,' came the reply, followed by, 'Oo oo oo,' more stridently and then a jocular, 'Oo oo oo.'

'Woof woof woof woof woof. Woof?'

'Oo oo oo oo.'

'Woof Woof? Woof woof!'

'Oo,' said Monkey Man, and then he shook his head and corrected himself and said, 'Oo,' and added, 'Oo.'

'Woof!' laughed The Growl, before adding, 'Woof?'

'Oo,' said Monkey Man.

The Growl was pleasantly astonished by this. 'Woof woof.' He began to feel an affection for the hairy fella.

'Oo oo oo,' sighed Monkey Man, and then, 'Oo.'

Doug scratched his head.

He looked at Russell, who asked Hardy, 'What are they saying? I thought you said you were going to interpret the conversation for us? Why don't you do so? We can't understand them at all.'

Hardy shrugged, which wasn't easy when laced inside a papoose. 'Don't blame me. They aren't saying anything intelligible. They are just making *woof* and *oo* sounds at each other.'

Doug said, 'We came a long way for nothing much.'

Russell disagreed. 'Just looking at that house up there, a paddle steamer in the treetops, made it worthwhile.'

'Do you think we can climb up and go inside?'

'Let's ask permission.'

But Hardy answered with sad eyes, 'Sorry, only Monkey Man and myself are allowed in the manor.' He lowered his voice to a whisper but projected it so skilfully that they could still hear him clearly. 'To be honest, we have guests in the house at present. Showgirls. There's a chess tournament taking place. Don't care to be disturbed at such times.'

'That's a shame.'

'But I'm sure we can entertain you down here, if you don't mind hanging around at ground level. After all, you are guests too, even if you aren't quite as alluring as chess-playing showgirls.'

'I could really do with a cup of tea,' said Russell.

Hardy nodded. 'Househelp!'

'Who are you calling?' asked Doug.

'The househelp. A set of mechanical servants that Monkey Man bought in a strange shop in New Orleans a long time ago. He bought them from a peculiar fella named Gunsmith Ghouls.'

'Astonishing,' commented Russell.

'Yes, Monkey Man used them to drag the paddle steamer all the way from the Mississippi River and then hoist it into the trees using ropes and pulleys. It was a tough job but those mechanical servants never tire. They sometimes rust or pop a rivet but they never sleep.'

And now into the glade that wasn't a glade trundled and stalked a bunch of curiously rendered metal men. They were all of different shapes and sizes and a few were three times the height and girth of a normal person. Most had strong arms but others had tentacles or tendrils. They began setting up a vast cauldron on the other side of the small clearing. Then they lit a fire under it and filled the cauldron with water and tea leaves.

Russell licked his lips in anticipation.

The Growl and Monkey Man finally finished their conversation. Both of them looked satisfied, triumphant even, though below the smugness there was a hint of bewilderment in the eyes of each.

The Growl turned to his companions and said, 'I asked him if he was truly the quickest draw in the West.'

'What did he say?' wondered Doug.

'I don't know but I believe him anyway. Just look at the muscles in those arms of his! I am very impressed.'

Hardy now said, 'Look here, dog-face, I'm still a bit upset at the way you killed my companion, Randall.'

The Growl seemed embarrassed, but the cowl put his blushes in the shade and when he spoke it was in a firm tone. 'I'm sorry about that, pard. It was in the nature of an accident, if you recall.'

'What are you talking about?' wondered Doug.

The Growl was morose.

'Something that happened back in California

quite a while ago. It doesn't matter much, but I did a noble deed and unfortunately this fella's friend ended up with a broken skull and a squashed brain. His name was Randall. That's all. I'm not surprised Hardy is upset.'

'It was a terrible death,' said Hardy, 'almost as gruesome as the demise of that stupid editor in St Louis.'

The atmosphere of the glade suddenly chilled.

'Beg your pardon, pard?'

That was The Growl speaking. His eyes narrowed.

Hardy laughed and said:

'Before I met you, doggy, I was part of a gang. We came together for one job and killed a newspaper editor.'

'Was his name Ridley Smart, by any chance?'

'Yes, it was. How did you know that? Hey, I don't suppose you were his friend or something like that?'

The Growl muttered to himself, 'Two left,' and then the gun was in his gloved left hand and he had fired six bullets in succession. The bullets struck the trunk of the tree behind Monkey Man and ricocheted and five of them cut the strings that bound the papoose to Monkey man's back and the sixth made a hole in the centre of Hardy's forehead. 'One left now,' said The Growl and he glared at the tumbling papoose and the corpse inside it. His gun was empty and smoke issued in wisps from the barrel.

The papoose hit the ground with a thud.

Monkey Man roared.

He didn't understand why The Growl had killed Hardy. All he knew was that his interpreter had been shot by interlopers, and when interlopers interfere in the life cycle of an interpreter, that's when action must be taken. He jumped down from the branch and landed on his feet, but he rolled over anyway, stood in a crouch when the roll was finished, drew the bananas from his holsters in a flash so fast that ordinary flashes looked tardy in comparison, not that anyone present was actually comparing them, then lunged and stabbed The Growl in the chest with them. Banana pulp spurted.

'He really *is* fast,' said The Growl in admiration.

Russell stepped forwards.

'Don't!' warned Doug, but it was too late.

Russell was saying, 'There's no need for fighting and bloodshed. Look at me. I lost my ears some time ago and I know what deprivation means. My nose is falling off too! Well, the beings who exist on this planet are like the features of a face, a gigantic face, the visage of a god or goddess, and when they die, it's the same as if noses and lips and cheeks had fallen off, never to be put back on. I am pleading with you to see sense!'

Monkey Man picked him up with one hand, tossed him high into the air, and when he came down he kicked him.

This kick propelled Russell in a graceful arc across the glade. He probably would have landed on the leaf-strewn ground and survived with only a dozen or so bruises, but unfortunately the cauldron was in the way. It was bubbling now and Russell was headed straight for it.

'You will drown in the tea!' bellowed Doug.

'No, he'll scald to death first,' said The Growl, 'and won't get a chance to indulge the luxury of drowning.'

'I think you are right,' conceded Doug.

As Russell flew through the air, he heaved a sigh of resignation and gazed at his erstwhile companions sadly.

Then he spoke to them as follows:

'I don't have much time to tell you. But I would regret it forevermore if I didn't make the effort. I just want to say that if I had studied under a shaman for months, as you lot did, I wouldn't want to be turned into any animal. Not a dog or badger or monkey. No thanks! Not that I have anything against animals and the truth is that I adore them. But that's not the point. No, I mean that I would prefer to be turned, if at all possible, into –

'What?' cried The Growl.

'Get to the point,' yelled Doug.

'That's good advice,' said Russell, 'because there's not enough time to waste when one is flying through the air, so I ought to be very concise, and in fact when I think about it more deeply, I realise that I only have a few seconds to say anything at all, and all this faffing around is using up those seconds at a terrific rate, and that simply won't do.'

'It won't do,' agreed Doug.

'I second that,' affirmed The Growl.

'Well, then,' said Russell, 'let me at least attempt to convey what I want to say more efficiently than I have managed so far. I would prefer, after a lengthy period of studying the shamanic arts, to be turned not into an animal, which is usually what happens, if I understand correctly, nor into a vegetable or mineral, which is impossible anyway, according to your best information on the matter, but into something else. A biscuit.'

'A biscuit!' cried Doug.

'Biscuits aren't animals,' said The Growl sadly, 'and your request would be refused. Sorry. But you never need to know that. You have just landed in the tea and are being boiled to death. If you *were* a biscuit, it might have helped, I imagine, but you aren't. Nonetheless I shall bear your words in mind and think of you as a biscuit. That's the least I can do for your memory. You were going to die soon anyway. The powder in the jar seemed to be poisonous. Perhaps in the future scientists will rediscover it and explain why it shouldn't be handled. Until then, dunk in peace, my friend.'

Monkey Man turned on his heel and glowered at The Growl. The fight was certain to continue and nobody could reliably say who might win, for they were both hardened warriors of the Old West, but just at that moment, a voice called from high above, from the treetops.

A showgirl was leaning out of one of the paddle

steamer's portholes and she was bare-chested. 'Are you coming back to finish the game? I just made an *en passant* move and took your pawn and now Dolores is trying out the Sicilian Defence for the very first time.'

Another bare-chested woman leaned out of the next porthole. 'That's right, Maisy, and Annie is just about to castle on the queen's rook's side, it's getting so exciting I can scarcely breathe.'

'A queenside castling!' gasped Maisy.

'You bet!' said Annie, a third bare-chested showgirl leaning out of a third porthole and giggling sweetly.

Dolores said, 'It's going to be beautiful and as smooth as silk underwear. I can't wait to see it performed.'

Monkey Man took note of these alluring words and with a very loud grunt he forsook his desire for combat and raced up the tree with astounding agility, returning to his manor in the sky.

The Growl looked at Doug and said:

'Time to hit the road.'

Doug looked around. 'No road around here. It's a trackless way through a mighty forest.' He paused. 'But I know what you mean. At least I think I do. I reckon I'll stay with you until you find and kill the last man on your list. Then we can say goodbye properly.'

'Be a pleasure to have your company.'

'Likewise, buddy.'

The dog-man and the badger-man mounted their

horses and rode away. As for Russell's horse, it was free to go wherever it liked. It approached the boiling cauldron, sniffed the man-flavoured tea, shook its head and trotted on. Cries of delight came from high above. A few banana skins floated down and joined the pile of them already amassed in the glade. One day Fate itself would come here and slip on those skins. Wait and see!

Chapter Seven
Sideliners

The infamous gunslinger known as Bat Rattan was preparing for a shoot-out against the equally fabled Kirk Doings in the town of Stair Creek and they both stood in the dusty main street and faced each other. It was sunset and squinting was unnecessary, but they squinted.

'Gonna fill you full of lead,' said Bat Rattan.

'Fill me full of bread?'

'I said lead, not bread. Why the hell would I want to fill you full of bread? Do I look like some kind of baker to you? Hell, boy, that's another insult I must add to your considerable tally.'

'Huh? To my formidable alley?'

'I said considerable, not formidable, and I said tally, not alley. Something is wrong with your ears, boy!'

'Beers ahoy? What does that mean?'

Bat Rattan glowered.

But Kirk Doings was genuinely confused. People always assumed he was a joker, deliberately misunderstanding words for the purpose of mockery, but he wasn't. There really was something odd about his understanding. It got him into fights and because he was fabled he usually made a messy myth of his opponents, but in this case he was well-matched.

Bat Rattan was the smoothest, slickest, most accurate quick draw in Utah and Kirk Doings was the slickest, smoothest, most precise shooter in Nevada. They had chosen Stair Creek as good neutral territory for the combat. People watched from windows and doorways but had no intention of interfering. Even the sheriff kept at a safe distance.

The moment of destiny was approaching. Bat Rattan's hand inched down to his holster and his squint became a cold glare. Then something very strange happened. A large hand on the end of an immeasurably long arm came down the street at high speed. The fingers were spread wide and the palm of this bizarre hand connected with Bat Rattan's sternum. It pushed him along and he whizzed through the dust, always accelerating.

Kirk Doings removed his hat and fanned himself. He was surprised. This impossible arm was none of his doing. Bat Rattan was cursing and screaming as he vanished in a puff of distance.

The arm was moving at a tremendous rate now. Bat Rattan was vanishing over the horizon, he was nothing more than a dot, then he was nothing at all. It was the strangest occurrence in the history of Stair Creek. The arm was moving so fast now it was a blur. Kirk Doings turned away and pushed through the door of the saloon. He ordered a beer.

'That didn't end the way I was expecting,' he told the barman, as he took a huge gulp of the amber liquid.

'It happens that way sometimes, I guess.'

'The West is weird.'

The arm in question belonged to one of the members of a very unusual gang of outlaws. They weren't really outlaws, nor were they vigilantes, but they liked to think of themselves as bad guys.

They called themselves The Sideliners and there were four of them. They sought to 'sideline' people by removing them from the action, any action at all that might be happening, by pushing them out of the frame of an event with one of their peculiar extendable arms.

They stood on a revolving steel platform and this is how they were able to reach out to any part of the United States without turning their own bodies. The platform at the moment was located in Minnesota but it was able to slide in any direction over the ground. In fact it hovered several feet in the air and the reason it did this was because the gang members were futurists and they believed that levitation was the best way forward.

However, the hovering of the platform was accomplished by trickery rather than technology. The platform was mounted on the backs of several horses. To perfect the illusion, the horses were rendered transparent by rays emitted from an invisibility projector, a device they had obtained years earlier. They liked to be reminded of the future. They were brothers, two pairs of identical twins, and their names were anagrams of each other.

One was called Cher Tahoe, another was called Echo Harte, the third was called Hoe Rachet, the fourth was called Rhee Tacho. These are unusual names but it has already been explained they are all anagrams of 'each other'. Maybe the parents of the gang had enjoyed puzzles. Many people do. But the question remains as to why they did what they did? What was the actual point of pushing folks out of the frame of the action?

The question is unanswerable. Even The Sideliners didn't know why. The best they could say in their defence was that everyone needs a hobby. And the hobby they had chosen for themselves was to regard the West as a fiction, just a story, and to first push characters they didn't like into the margins and then over the edge of the page into oblivion.

Oblivion was the presumed destination of anyone who had been sidelined in this fashion, but there were hints that sometimes a sidelined character would return to the exact spot where he had been pushed away. These hints consisted of the fact that occasionally unknown marksmen took potshots at the brothers. It was assumed that the sidelined personages were seeking revenge. So far, none of The Sideliners had been wounded.

The brothers picked on random individuals. If you had a reputation, good or bad, they were more likely to target you. But they often pushed inoffensive nobodies out of the story of reality too. They were just another hazard of life in a risky time in a perilous place. After they had sidelined a person, the owner of the arm that had done the deed would rest for a week. Stretching even the most flexible arm thousands of miles is hard work. He would lie on a soft couch and drink coffee and nibble spicy snacks.

The Growl and Doug were riding through Washington State, a part of the nation unknown to them. They had an idea that if they visited every state one by one, it would mean they were bonded to the country in such a severe way that the land itself would assist them in their quest.

The quest was simply to find the final killer of The Growl's boss, Ridley Smart, and maybe even learn *why* he had been murdered. And after that? Doug was fearful that The Growl would fall to pieces, psychologically speaking, when he had discharged his urge for vengeance. A life needs a purpose and there was nothing The Growl loved enough to fill the void when the final piece of the mission was put in place. Doug puffed his cheeks.

He was about to tackle the subject once again with The Growl when, from nowhere, an object rammed into him and pushed him off his horse. He slumped on the ground but he wasn't allowed to stay there for long. The object pushed at him more firmly and he slid away very quickly. The Growl's gun was already in his gloved hand, but he didn't shoot.

He first wanted to know *what* he was shooting at. All he saw was a lateral blur, something pinkish, and his friend being pushed along the ground at a very dangerous speed. The friction burned his trousers and smoke rose from the seat of his pants, but already he was dwindling and the smoke was dispersing. When smoke disperses, avengers dispute with themselves, and that's what The Growl did right now. He frowned profoundly.

While he watched, Doug disappeared forever and the blur vanished too, an opportunity to take action wasted. Now there was nothing *to* aim at. Shaking his head sorrowfully, The Growl muttered a fond farewell to his erstwhile comrade. He had enjoyed riding with a badger-man. They had explored a lot of the West, a fine working holiday it had been.

The Growl had spent a long time on his own. Before he had met Doug his life had included a lot of solitude. So it was easy enough for him to return to his previous condition. He kept riding, mystified by what had happened but hardly worried about it. His focus was on finding the final killer of his former boss, or at the very least learning the fella's name and general whereabouts. Thus it was a shock when he too was assaulted by a hand on the end of an enormous arm. It seemed to arrive from nowhere.

But the way he was pushed out of his saddle wasn't quite the same as the way Doug had been. The Growl's reactions were faster. He leaped up from his saddle, determined not to be flung onto the ground by the hand. His plan was to cling to the lowest branch of the tree above him. But his fingers were unable to secure a grip and the hand kept pushing him. He drew his gun and fired into the wrist and forearm of his attacker.

He chipped the bone of that monstrous arm and now it bent upwards at a slight angle. The result of this wound was that The Growl was pushed not only laterally, as Doug had been, but vertically too. The angle of ascent was about 10 degrees or so, not very steep but quite sufficient to put him among the clouds in a minute or so, because the speed of the arm was incredible. He was helpless to resist the force that propelled him.

Over the forest canopy he rose and the view was tremendous. He could see the ocean far away in one direction, and in the other direction he could observe clearly the long arm, many miles of it, but the shoulder it was connected to was hidden by the curvature of the planet. Wisps of cloud brushed his face. Higher and higher he went, and further along too. He was over the sea now, the coast of his homeland was receding rapidly.

Although it had been a warm summer's day on the ground, it grew chilly up here and The Growl felt a pain in his chest. He realised he was being pushed up into regions of the atmosphere too thin for him to breathe. Soon enough he would lose consciousness, and be dead a few minutes after that, and therefore his boss would never be avenged.

His gun was empty and all the magic he knew was insufficient to give him an edge, unless he again turned himself into a pack of playing cards and floated back down to the ground, but that option carried its own perils. The cards might scatter over a wide area and he would be unable to reassemble himself fully. He would be missing an arm or an ear or his tail. He would rather die in one piece, he decided, like a good noble dog.

The Growl considered if he ought to speak some memorable last words. It didn't seem worth it. There was no one to memorise them. The arm had no ears and neither did the shimmering clouds. He satisfied himself by growling at the place in the sky where the moon was, though it was scarcely visible in daylight. That was his epitaph for himself.

But The Growl didn't die. A trillion to one chance saved him. A circular object was approaching, and as it neared him he saw how large it was, a vehicle of an outlandish design. It seemed to spot him and kept pace with the arm, so that as far as he was concerned it was motionless. It made curious beeping noises. At last a ray of green light shot out from it and enveloped him. He felt himself in the grip of a force even stronger than the hand. The hand continued to push but now the green ray was battling it.

They were struggling for possession of his body, and with it, his soul, and although he didn't know it at the time, he was being rescued by a flying saucer. It was a remarkable coincidence that one should be passing just at that moment. Of course, they weren't called flying saucers back then, but celestial hats, and it was generally reckoned they originated on other planets, maybe Mars or Venus or the planets of some distant star.

The truth of the matter is that they were from the future. They were flying time machines. The inhabitants of the future Earth conducted occasional jaunts into their own past in order to conduct research and have a bit of a good time. It wasn't the first time they had abducted a cowboy, but it *was* the first time they'd taken a pupil of a shaman who had partly turned himself into a dog and wore a cowl in order to conceal his muzzle.

The Growl was gradually wrenched away from the hand. Pull had emerged victorious over push. The ray sucked him through a circular hatch that suddenly opened in the side of the vessel. He was deposited on a metal floor. Then reality blurred and shrieked. The engines had been shifted up a gear. The flying saucer was returning to its own century. The journey took only several minutes. Then it gently touched down on an obsidian platform in the middle of a bizarre city. The Growl was stupefied as he stared through the portholes. Towers of immense size and weird shapes, elevated walkways, strange beings floating through the air on concentric circles of visible magnetism.

The hatch in the side of the vehicle opened again, the ramp tilted and down he rolled into the future of his planet. He assumed he was on another world. But now a friendly face beamed down at him and it beamed down literally. It began as motes of radiated energy and rapidly coalesced into a solid object. A colossal head mounted on twenty tiny legs.

'Greetings, ancestor,' said the huge mouth.

The Growl frowned.

He picked himself up, dusted himself down and discovered there wasn't a speck of dust on him. This city was abnormally clean. He smiled and chuckled and shook his head disbelievingly.

'Well, I'll be darned. A metal man! I have seen plenty of man beasts who came out of caves in which shamans were living, but I never saw a living man who was metal all over and had the gift of speech. At least, I am assuming you *are* a man? If not, what are you?'

'I am a robot. I am from the future. We rescued you from that really long arm and the hand on the end of it. You were brought here for study, but taking a closer look at you, I don't think we can learn much. It is our duty to return you to your own time, and we will.'

'Don't meet your expectations, huh?'

'You could put it like that, I suppose. We never really know quite what we are going to end up with when we abduct an ancestor. It's a lottery, a process of pick and mix. We picked badly.'

'You are very blunt, metal head.'

'True. I am a logical machine. But please call me Hugo. That is my proper name and the metal I am made from is an alloy that won't be discovered by your kind for another 150 years. Like I said, you are not precisely what we require. It happens this way often enough.'

'What's wrong with me?' asked The Growl.

'To be honest, you pong a bit. I mean, I was expecting a human from our past to be a bit whiffy but you –'

'I am part dog, that's why,' said The Growl.

'True. Nonetheless –'

'What's the year now?' demanded The Growl.

'100010010100,' said Hugo.

'Hey, that's mighty far into the future, ain't it?'

'Not especially. That's the year in binary, which is the number system of the robots who are in charge. In your own number system the year is 2196, two hundred years into your future.'

The Growl digested this with a low whistle and he slowly gazed around at the architecture and the inhabitants of the city. The structures defied gravity and so did the citizens. Some of the towers and arches weren't even attached to the ground. The Growl watched with a blend of apprehension and pleasure as they bobbed higher and lower, shifting position constantly. Meanwhile, more flying saucers came in to land on other obsidian platforms scattered throughout what was visible to him of the city.

'It's so *futuristic*, but I guess that's to be expected.'

Hugo considered this. 'That's right, but one day all of this will come to be seen as hopelessly old-fashioned.'

'One day? What day might that be?'

'Decades hence.'

'Can't you be more precise?'

'Does not compute.'

'What the hell does that mean?'

'It means that I am unable to work it out. I am a robot and thus excellent at computing things, but what you asked me doesn't compute. That means it was a bad idea that you asked it in the first place. You shouldn't ask questions like that because they cause trouble.'

'What kind of trouble?' wondered The Growl.

'Our circuits overheat.'

The Growl made a wry face and Hugo added, 'Look here, modelling the future is a notoriously tricky thing to do using mathematics. Most models get it wrong because there are too many variables involved. That's why we never try or try only very occasionally.'

'But can you model the past well?'

'Absolutely. We are great at doing that, it's something we can do with our eyes closed. We can model *your* present to an accuracy that truly is remarkable. We know almost everything about your own time in terms of probabilities, even though we still wish to study you to increase our understanding of your mental processes. The past is simple.'

'But isn't the future just the past in reverse?'

'No, not really.'

The Growl said, 'I think it is.'

'Well, it isn't.'

'Yeah? I say it is.'

'I say it isn't.'

'Is,' snarled The Growl, and he was dismayed when Hugo responded with a very childish, 'Isn't.'

The Growl flared his nostrils.

'I am biological and mystical. I don't care to argue with an artificial dude. The real is superior to the synthetic.'

Hugo said, 'Are you absolutely certain you aren't synthetic yourself? Let me tell you a story. There was once a man who, at the age of forty, played with his belly button in the bath. He pressed it and his chest swung open on hinges. His chest was a hatch! Inside there were wires and cogs. He was simply a robot all along, one who had been constructed only the previous month. Those forty years of his experience and memories were nothing more than an illusion, part of his programming. What he had always assumed was the external cosmos was in fact only his software reality.'

'I'm safe, I don't take baths,' said The Growl.

'None of us are safe!'

'Pard, there's no way I'm a robot. You said that I smell bad. That's strong evidence I'm organic. But suppose I *am* a robot, suppose my odour can also be programmed. What happens to my consciousness when I break, when I cease to function? What happens to my mind?'

'That depends on whether you were based on another sapient being or not. If you weren't, then you will snap into oblivion, nothing more. But if you were, you'll reassume your original identity.'

'The illusion will be stripped away and reality will manifest itself?'

'Yes, unless the new reality is another illusion.'

'Layers and layers of existence?'

'Why not? And none are necessarily more valid than any other. Even the lowest reality can be regarded as equal to the highest because it is *true* to those who inhabit it. This is a friendly warning. Don't assume too much about what you are. Your personal history and memories can be programmed into you. We live in our own software worlds.'

'All of us? Including you?'

'I am a robot. I was always a robot.'

'You don't seem much of a robot to me, sorry, pard. I mean, I didn't even know what a robot was until half an hour ago, but it is obvious to me that if a robot's job is to compute but you say "it doesn't compute" then you aren't what might be called a shining example of the breed, irrespective of whether the past is the future backwards or not.'

'That is incorrect. You knew what robots were before you arrived here. You encountered them in the form of Monkey Man's mechanical servants. Not all robots are electronic, some are clockwork. You are also wrong about how good I am at computing. I'm the best.'

'You're the best? Do you like gambling, pard? I bet that's one computation you've already got wrong!'

The giant head seemed very upset at this. The Growl noticed and because he had a soft heart, he added:

'Sorry, Hugo.'

'I bet I'm much better at computing than you'll ever be,' blubbered Hugo as his metal lips quivered.

'A challenge, huh?' asked The Growl.

'Not exactly, no, but –'

'I accept!' snapped The Growl and in a flash his gun was in his hand. 'I'm going to ask you to compute how many bullets are left in my Colt Walker. Here is the weapon in question.'

'Oh, come now, I really don't –'

'Too difficult for you, huh? Well, Hugo, I am willing to give you a clue. I will let you know the answer, but in a sum that you must compute. *Then* we'll see if you're as good as you claim. Are you ready? Here's the sum. The number of bullets left in my revolver is equal to nine times twenty-nine divided by three plus four minus thirteen times forty divided by five plus three plus twenty. In your own time. I'll be waiting.'

Hugo said, 'Let's be clear. You mean 9(29/3+4)-13(40/5+3)+20?'

'Sure,' said The Growl.

'Zero!' announced the robot head instantly.

The Growl frowned. 'Huh? That's right. But let me double check. Let me see now. Nine times twenty-nine is 261, divided by three is 87, plus four is 91, minus thirteen is 78, times forty is 3120, divided by five is 624, plus three is 627, plus twenty is 647. Huh? How can it be six hundred and forty-seven? The chamber only holds six rounds!'

'You didn't follow the correct order of operations. You didn't follow the rules known in your own time as BODMAS. That word is a mnemonic giving the correct order, which is brackets, order, division, multiplication, addition, and subtraction. The answer is zero.'

'Well, yeah, it *is* zero. But I still don't get it. Don't you just do the figuring as you go along? You mean you have to wait to hear the whole equation before you can start computing it? That doesn't sound too clever, pard. I was thinking you would do better than that.'

'I solved the problem. You have lost.'

'Hugo, I resent that.'

'What do you mean? How can you resent it?'

'Just do, that's all.'

The Growl aimed his gun at Hugo and cried, 'Lucky for you that my gun really is empty, otherwise –'

As a demonstration, he squeezed the trigger.

There was a detonation.

The barrel spat a bullet between Hugo's eyes.

'What the hell?'

The Growl was shocked. He ran to Hugo, who was teetering on his little feet. The robot was smoking from the cracks between his panels. Then with an oddly pitched gasp, he fell over.

'Hugo, I'm sorry, pard! The gun was empty.'

'Yes, it *was*,' said Hugo.

'Then where did the bullet come from?'

Hugo dribbled oil.

'You forgot that you are in your future now. When you calculated a total of 647 bullets, the tiny invisible robots that are everywhere in the air went to work and adjusted your gun to hold that many. Then it made those bullets and loaded them. Tiny invisible robots manipulate matter at the molecular level here. That's how we manage to live so well.'

'I just didn't know. Please forgive me!'

'Nothing to forgive.'

'Can't those tiny invisible robots fix you? Aren't they able to repair such injuries as you have sustained?'

'Well, it's a funny thing, but medicine is the one thing they *can't* do. Not sure why that should be, but that's the way it is. The original programmers just forgot, I guess. My death is certain and even though I am a robot I might still be reincarnated in some other form.'

'Another robot, you mean?' cried The Growl.

'A teapot probably.'

There was an uncomfortable pause.

'Hugo,' said The Growl, 'I never really got to know you well and I regret that. I don't even know if you have a surname. Well, do you? I know you think I stink, but we could have been buddies anyway. If circumstances were different, I mean. If you lived in my time.'

'We don't have surnames. We have evolved beyond them. I suppose you are worried about how you will get home? Please put your fears to rest. There are others here who will help you.'

'I'm mighty obliged, pard,' said The Growl.

'Anything else?'

'What do you mean?'

'Is there anything else I can do for you before I am gone? I have enough energy left for a last request.'

The Growl leaned closer. 'There is one thing. I don't suppose you are able to compute the identity of the tenth gunman who killed my boss? You said you were able to model the past.'

'Nothing easier! The answer to your question is a personage who is known as Gunsmith Ghouls. He's the one.'

'I have heard the name several times. But is it a pseudonym? Does he have a real name, this Gunsmith Ghouls?

'Yes, he does.'

'What is it?'

'Bodmas … It's a coincidence.'

'Bodmas what?'

'Bodmas Coincidence. Imagine! That's another coincidence.'

'Strange name. Not surprised he changed it to Gunsmith Ghouls. I changed my own name, you know that?'

'Of course we know. You were once Boll Bines.'

'Bill Bones, pard.'

'My apologies. We can model the past that is your present with excellent accuracy, indeed to twenty-nine decimal places, but your name clearly required modelling to thirty decimal places. Ah well. Too bad. Farewell. It is unlikely we will meet again, but who knows?'

'Well, don't you know? You are the robot around here, the one with a brain that can compute complex stuff.'

'I don't know,' said Hugo, and he died.

The Growl sighed.

Another robot head materialised next to the prone Hugo. This robot had an extra mouth on his forehead, three noses that constantly twitched, and four eyes. Both mouths spoke at the same time and they made a pleasant harmony, but one of them started coughing and The Growl had to strain his excellent ears to make out what the other mouth said.

'I am Ralph, I have been given the task of returning you to your own time. Please accompany me to the saucer over there. I know much about you. Once, a companion of yours rode by your side on a wagon pulled by a giant teapot. Now you have experienced saucer flight too. The only item missing in order to create a perfect teatime scene is a cup.'

'Don't care about any of that, pard.'

Ralph nodded. 'Then follow. My saucer awaits. Hugo told me you are half dog? Is that why you stink so?'

'Kinda rude to speak like that,' said The Growl.

'My apologies,' said Ralph. Then he added in an undertone, 'But by heck you do honk quite a bit. Phew!'

'I am organic, so what do you expect? And I'm not as smelly as my friend Doug, who was recently pushed by a hand on the end of a very long arm out of my life forever. An arm almost identical to the one that pushed me into the sky. What exactly *are* those arms?'

'Just arms. The clue is in the word,' said Ralph.

'Come on, pard. They must be more than that. No ordinary arm can stretch itself hundreds or even thousands of miles. They are supernatural arms, for sure. I am extra sensitive to magic.'

'The arms belong to a gang called The Sideliners. You don't need to worry about them. I can reveal that they are on the verge of their own destruction. It is going to be a very ironic demise.'

'How so?' asked The Growl with a frown.

Ralph smiled and said:

'In a few days from now, they will accidentally sideline themselves. Their arms are stretching right now, seeking new targets but missing everyone. They are stretching them further and further.

Eventually their arms will stretch right around the world. Yes, a full circumnavigation of the planet will be completed by those arms. Then the hands will touch their own bodies and they will push, push with misplaced glee, push harder than they have ever pushed before, and that's how they will push themselves out of the action. Sidelined for all time. I am telling you all this because I think it's what Hugo would have wanted. Poor Hugo, my best friend! A tragedy.'

'I am sorry,' said The Growl very softly.

They reached a saucer on an obsidian platform. Ralph ushered The Growl up the ramp and a hatch opened to allow them both to enter. Ralph indicated a comfortable chair for The Growl.

'Unless you'd prefer to curl up in a basket?'

The Growl frowned.

Was Ralph mocking him? He studied the robot head carefully and decided not. But it was difficult to tell.

The hatch closed and the saucer lifted.

The voyage was smooth.

'Shall I deposit you where you came from?'

The Growl nodded.

Then he had a sudden thought. 'No! Take me elsewhere. Drop me off near a city called New Orleans.'

'Sure, I can do that,' said Ralph.

The Growl grinned and his bared fangs shone in the unnatural interior glow of the flying saucer. Once he reached New Orleans in his own time, the ultimate part of his revenge could begin. The seeking and killing of his final target. But it was going to be difficult. The guy he was after was quite a different proposition from the others. He was dangerous and strange and very clever, a man who sold peculiar objects and contraptions.

Would he sell The Growl peace of mind?

Or would it have to be taken by force? The Growl suspected the latter case would apply. He licked his lips.

The sun would soon set on his quest.

A blood red climax!

Chapter Eight
Gunsmith Ghouls

The Growl wandered the streets of New Orleans and he stood out rather like a sore thumb, but luckily for him sore thumbs were the order of the day. Every man and woman looked strange, even if they seemed beautiful on the outside, because there was some quality in the air that had changed them deep down. It wasn't the heat or the music or the clouds of spicy smoke that drifted along to plug nostrils, but a more mysterious mood, some ancient pulsation in the very fabric of the place. Not that it was really fabric, but stone and brick and iron, a city of elegance and savage impulses.

Finding a small and cheap hotel halfway along a narrow alley in the heart of the city, The Growl paid for a room and he sat on the edge of his bed and he considered how best to proceed. What did he know about Gunsmith Ghouls? It wasn't very much, that's for sure. The fella owned a store that sold curios. He was merciless. But this didn't mean that he sold knicknacks ruthlessly. No, he liked to spread chaos throughout the world. Clockwork cats were the least of it. He might be an adept in the occult arts. What if he turned out to be even more magically strong than a desert shaman?

Rushing into anything wouldn't be a wise move, The Growl decided. His patience ought to be cultivated and a careful plan should be devised. He sighed and went out to find a restaurant. He needed a meal and a drink. He was in one of the most unusual cities on the continent, a place where French was spoken as often as English, perhaps more often. He tried to remember what little he knew of the language. He would get by somehow. Trumpet music followed him and it also preceded him. He didn't mind in the least. People enjoyed life here, but the question remained: what kind of life?

He found a small establishment selling crêpes. He studied the menu. Yes, crêpes were the only thing available here, but they came in many varieties. He wouldn't be disappointed. *Crêpes sucrées et crêpes salées*. He pondered. It was a difficult choice. *Crêpes Suzette*? or the more Americanised *Crêpes Susannah* (with a *brulée* banjo on its knee)? He decided to order all kinds and judge their differences later. He was famished. Travelling to the future and back had given him an appetite. Having made his order, he gazed out of the window but there wasn't much to see in the narrow lane.

The Sideliners were still alive and active, but soon enough they would be responsible for their own destruction. That's what he had been told by a giant trustworthy robot head, so there was no need to seek them out and put a stop to their doings. He missed Doug, though! Better to concentrate on finding the last killer of his former boss. The waiter came and deposited plates of *crêpes* on the table, mounds and mountains of them.

'That was quick!' cried The Growl appreciatively.

'*Désolé monsieur. Bien que je vous comprenne, je veux prétendre que non. Je suis un homme rusé,*' said the waiter.

'Oh, yes.' The Growl struggled with his memory. '*Bon! Mais ma capacité à parler français est comme la capacité d'un cactus à jouer aux échecs avec des showgirls. Je suis désolé, s'il vous plaît.*'

'Showgirls, monsieur?'

'*Danseurs. Avec de longues jambes et des bas érotiques.*'

'*Oui! J'aime beaucoup!*'

The strain of thinking in a language he barely spoke exhausted The Growl and he growled. If only the waiter spoke Dog! But even if he did, it was likely he would only speak French dog, a type of lingo called Poodle, rather than the plain honest Dog that The Growl knew. It didn't matter. He knew some magic. It would take away half his energy but he could perform a spell that turned all the French he heard in New Orleans into a type of English. He closed his eyes and forced his mind through the tortuous passages in the labyrinth of the spell and when he finished, an hour had passed. But the waiter was in no particular rush for him to vacate the premises.

'Take as much time as you like,' he told The Growl. 'This isn't one of those horrible fast food canteens.'

He was speaking in French but The Growl heard it as English, accented in a strange way, of course, but easily understandable. He nodded and smiled and ordered more *crêpes*. When they came, just seconds later, he asked, 'Your speed is amazing. You say that this isn't a "fast food" place but I have never known a restaurant to serve food so promptly. This *crêperie* is more efficient even than a military chuck wagon. I don't get it.'

'We use a special machine to prepare them. It is a very advanced device, a unique contraption. It cooks the *crêpes* with beams of energy derived from gems such as rubies and half-silvered mirrors. I'm not sure of the theory behind it but I regard it as utterly marvellous.'

'Where did you obtain such a device?'

'From a curio shop right here in New Orleans. The man who provided it was called Gunsmith Ghouls. He refused to reveal where it originally came from. I am a discreet personage and I didn't push him for details. The contraption now stands in a corner of the kitchen.'

At the words 'push him' The Growl shuddered, thinking of The Sideliners and their antics. Then he forced the thought from his head, concentrated on the present, and asked, 'Where is his shop located? It sounds like a very interesting place to visit. I would like to go.'

The waiter nodded. He remembered it well.

He told The Growl:

'Royal Street, the western end where it meets Franklin Avenue. The owner told us that he was preparing to sell the property and move away. He planned to sell it to some people who wanted to turn it into a coffee shop called Flora. He was tired of standing behind a counter all day. Also, he had a long fang that was once longer, or so he claimed. Every time he sells a curio, his fang shortens by half and one day it will be gone.'

'But he hasn't sold the shop just yet?'

'No, if you are lucky he'll still be there. You'd better hurry. It's not too far from here, fortunately for you.'

'Unfortunately for him,' muttered The Growl.

'I beg your pardon?'

'Nothing,' said The Growl. He paid for the *crêpes*, left a generous tip ('If you have aches in your knees, rub coconut oil and turmeric into them') and then he hurried out. Revenge is a puzzle and he was close to solving it. A few cross words with Gunsmith Ghouls and then he would draw on him and blast him to kingdom come, or republic come, considering there were no kingdoms here. He would complete his quest at last.

Gunsmith Ghouls stood behind his counter and he glanced at his shop, a hollow space with plenty of room to leap about, and he laughed. His fang was only two inches long now. There was one more item in his shop to be sold. When he had managed to get rid of it, his fang would be only one inch long, practically the same length as all his other teeth.

'I have waited so long!' he said to himself.

At the word 'long' he shuddered, remembering two things, the first being how long his fang once was, the second being the incredibly extended arm that had entered his shop one afternoon and tried to push him out of the frame of the action. Long things were abominable.

He hated and feared long things so much that he never even read novels if they had more than 250 pages. He shunned operas and spaghetti. He refused to play chess with showgirls and insisted on playing snakes and ladders instead but without the snakes. The ladders were fine because they were short. Longitude lines gave him the horrors and latitude lines he could only tolerate near one of the planet's two poles. Even the sentences he spoke were never long, except in very rare cases such as emergencies.

'Life is short!' he said to himself approvingly.

'Art is long,' he fumed.

'I am short,' he consoled himself.

The door creaked open.

The customer who entered was wearing a cowl. His hands were sheathed in white gloves. He walked with a stoop and the nose on the end of his face was in constant motion. He had a *long* face and Gunsmith Ghouls fought down his nausea as he gazed upon it. The customer inspected the items on display. This was an easy operation because all the items had been sold and were no longer there. Only one object remained on a shelf. It was a cowl. The Growl frowned at it and touched his own cowl gingerly.

'Good day,' said Gunsmith Ghouls. 'I see you are attracted by the cowl on display in my curio shop. You are touching your own cowl gingerly. It is nice to touch things gingerly because ginger is a beautiful flavour. But the cowl you see here is lemon, vanilla and strawberry.'

'Not really a very manly colour, is it?'

'True enough, I guess.'

'But that's OK because I ain't manly. I mean, I *am* manly partly, but I am also doggy. It's a nice cowl.'

Gunsmith Ghouls tried to keep his excitement from showing. If he sold this final curio, his teeth would be normal again and he would be free to wander the world without feeling like a freak.

'Woof, woof!' added The Growl suddenly.

'I beg your pardon?'

'I don't suppose you ever had a diving suit in stock? I have long wanted to put a diving suit on an insight.'

'Sold the last one a week ago. None left.'

'Just the cowl then?'

'Yes, but it's the best cowl ever made.'

'What exactly can it do?'

'Well, it works the same as an ordinary cowl. It conceals the face in a mass of shadows. Not impenetrable shadows but alluring ones. Penumbras rather than the darker umbrae of a mask.'

'My own cowl does that,' said The Growl.

'My cowl does more.'

'Sure, but *what*? I need to know quickly.'

'Yes, haste is good.'

'So tell me why it's so special?'

'When you wear it, people will think you are a gaucho.'

'Huh? What's that?'

'A cowboy from Argentina.'

The Growl laughed. 'You know something? I have been thinking about that country recently. Reckon I'll retire there. I had a friend from there and he told me. I am close to retirement.'

'Really? You seem awfully young. What do you do?'

'What? I am The Growl.'

'Yes, but is that actually a job?'

'It's a hobby and a calling. My hobby is to do jobs. I have one more job to do. It concerns you, funnily enough.'

Gunsmith Ghouls stood on tiptoe so that his frown could be clearly seen by this curious customer. 'How?'

The Growl stepped forward, opened his mouth and with his huge tongue he licked the face of the storekeeper, who spluttered and wiped the drool from his cheeks with his sleeves. 'Ugh!'

'It's commonly regarded as a sign of affection when a dog does that. But I don't feel affection for you, pard.'

'Who the hell are you?' bellowed Gunsmith Ghouls.

'The avenger of Ridley Smart!'

'Oh, him!' Gunsmith held his sides and laughed loudly. 'That prototype! I thought he was rubbish and needed to be decommissioned. He was making too many errors. He somehow managed to secure employment as the editor of some newspaper in St Louis and that was fine. But he began malfunctioning. He sent his reporters on some crazy missions! It would have ruined my reputation if he had continued getting more crazy.'

The Growl stepped back, his jaw slack.

'You mean that he –'

'A clockwork puppet,' said Gunsmith Ghouls.

'Like the cat you made?'

'Ah, so you know about the cat? Chasey, his name was. You didn't happen to fall into the clutches of Hermit Chumps, did you? He was a scoundrel, but the world is full of them. Too bad.'

'Yes, I did but he is no longer a scoundrel.'

'You reformed him?'

'A bullet did. But who cares about that madman? My editor was a puppet? Powered by clockwork, huh?'

'And chemicals. But wait, *your* editor?'

'That's what I said.'

'So you were a newspaperman?'

'Yes, I was. But I haven't been one for a long time. Not since I studied the occult arts with Tony the Shaman.'

'And now you are The Growl? You want to kill me because I killed your editor? But I didn't kill him. I hired a gang of nine others and we went to seek him out. We put him out of commission because he was faulty. He wasn't even alive in the first place. I hope you haven't hurt any of the nine innocent men in my gang? We did the right thing.'

The Growl panted with the enormity of the truth.

'I have killed all of them.'

'Oh, that's too bad, really it is! What a tragedy. Ah well, it can't be helped, I suppose. And you have come to kill me too? It is unnecessary, but if you feel you must, then go right ahead.'

Two six shooters appeared in The Growl's gloved hands. 'Too late to alter my plans now,' he said. 'Sorry.'

'I quite understand, dear boy. That's life.'

'Not for you, it isn't.'

Gunsmith inclined his head. 'True.'

'It's death,' said The Growl. Even as he spoke, he was acutely aware how unnecessary the words were.

'Just get it over with. I don't have all day.'

'You don't have *any* fraction of *any* day. Not now, you toothy villain who turns out not to be a villain –'

The Growl squeezed both triggers.

Both barrels jumped.

The two bullets struck Gunsmith Ghouls, one in the mouth and the other in the middle of his forehead. He toppled back immediately but there was no blood and The Growl was amazed to hear a twanging of springs. He stepped forwards, peered over the counter and gasped.

A smashed puppet!

Gunsmith Ghouls had been an automaton all along, a mannequin powered by clockwork and chemicals.

'Of all the lowdown tricks!' he snarled.

A voice interrupted him:

'Lowdown? Not at all. It was much safer to be a puppet than to be a living person. I would call that a sensible strategy, not a sneaky one. You would do the same thing, surely, if you could.'

The Growl blinked at a figure who was emerging from the rear of the shop. It was Gunsmith Ghouls. His fang gleamed in the dusty light that penetrated the grimy windows and his eyes twinkled.

'You constructed a puppet in your own likeness?'

'Not quite. I am a seller, not an inventor, but I do have a good mechanical head perched on my shoulders.'

'Yeah, I noticed that, pard.'

The Growl indicated the shattered head of the puppet, spilling cogs, wires, springs and oozing a thick oil.

Gunsmith Ghouls laughed appreciatively.

'Punslinger, huh?'

'It wasn't a pun. It was a play on words, yes, but not a pun. It's good to be precise when it comes to language.'

'That's the newspaperman in you, talking.'

'I am not Bill Bones.'

'So I gather. You are just The Growl.'

'Yes, I am, and do you know who you are? You're an explainer and you've got some explaining to do.'

'It's easy to tell. I don't design the puppets. They come to me in forms that are slightly different from the finished product. I fix them, adjust them, modify them. I have a good technical ability. For example, the cat Chasey came here in the form of an alarm clock. I adjusted him and made him what he was. And the same is true for all the others.'

'You turn alarm clocks into clockwork cats? Pard, to be honest, I think that is even *more* remarkable than if you had designed the cat from scratch. And as for your double here, what was he?'

'Before I modified him? A barometer, an egg whisk and a stock ticker. In fact most of the puppets have stock tickers inside them, plus various flasks and tubes of chemicals. Pendulums too.'

The Growl considered this. Finally he said:

'That's very interesting.'

'But?' snapped Gunsmith Ghouls, catching the inflection in The Growl's tone, the hint of determined menace.

'It won't save you.'

The two guns were in his gloved hands again. He squeezed the triggers. A flash from each barrel. The noise inside the confines of the shop was atrocious and his ears began ringing. He said:

'That's for Ridley Smart, even though he was just a puppet. He was still a good friend of mine. A fine fella.'

Gunsmith Ghouls fell back against the wall.

The shelf above him collapsed. The cowl on it came down too and landed near the feet of The Growl.

He studied it surreptitiously.

'That's really not a bad cowl at all,' he said to himself. He licked his lips. Would it hurt if he took it for himself? Plundering and looting was contrary to his nature and against his ethical code.

'Lemon, vanilla and strawberry,' he pondered.

He stooped lower.

Doubtless he would have picked it up, but a voice interrupted him. 'Nice to see you paying so much attention to my merchandise. I run a fabulous retail outlet here, I'm sure you'll agree.'

The Growl jerked upright and stared.

Gunsmith Ghouls was coming through the door at the rear of the shop, the third version of himself so far.

'You don't think I would be so foolish as to make only *one* copy of myself, do you? I am much more cautious than that. I am sorry to have outwitted you so easily. I was hoping you would prove to be a formidable opponent because I am bored being so clever and resourceful and never meeting my match. No matter! What will be, will be. Why don't you pay for the cowl honestly and watch as the fang in my head shrinks in half?'

'Why should I do that? You killed my boss!'

'And you killed me. Twice.'

'Yeah? Well, I got four more bullets in each of my guns and this time I am going to let you have two of each.'

'Your generosity is warped and savage.'

The Growl sneered.

'Is that so? Well, your nose and chin are warped and savage too, but you don't hear me complaining about 'em. Reckon I should shoot both of them off and do you some kind of favour.'

'Save your bullets. This is all pointless.'

'Say your prayers.'

'Why? I don't worship any god, so what's the point of saying my prayers? They aren't even my prayers but were written by someone else, long ago. Let me tell you something about that cowl on the floor. It's no ordinary garment. It is far more than it seems to be.'

'Distraction!' cried The Growl and he fired.

Twice with each hand.

Gunsmith Ghouls went down and more springs and cogs and oil spilled on the floor and The Growl sighed.

'Another puppet, darn it. When will it end?'

'Soon,' said a voice.

He looked up and saw Gunsmith Ghouls coming through the little door at the rear of the shop. But was this the real one? It was impossible to know from his exterior. The only way to be sure was to shoot him and see what happened. The Growl levelled his revolvers.

'I have two bullets left, one in each gun. I am

minded to shoot you first. If you turn out to be real, then my vengeance will be complete and with the second bullet I will end my own life.'

'But why? You have everything to live for!'

The Growl shook his head.

'No, I don't, not really. I have been considering the matter. Only the quest keeps me going. My existence has been aimless since I emerged from the cave. I learned a lot from Tony but I never learned how to truly bear the endless weight of reality, the crushing mass of the pressure of the universe. I look around me in the cities and towns I visit and I see people who wander automatically, without a sense of sincere purpose. In the wilderness, at night, I observe the stars and how they endure without any need to be watched. They burn but my soul has burned out. I am ashes below, just a husk.'

'Nonsense. That is the talk of a man who is weary, nothing more. You need a long rest. You have been tense. Your avenging mission has strung your nerves too tight. There is an easy answer.'

'What is it?'

'Buy the cowl, pay for it, watch my fang shrink to a normal size. Then turn and leave the shop. Never come back to it. A coffee shop it will be, anyway. The world is wide. What happened to your plans to retire to Argentina? Don't permit a sudden fit of depression to ruin everything. The cowl is something special. It's magical, not like your own cowl.'

The Growl frowned. He was sensitive to occult

vibrations, and yes, he was picking up emanations from the lemon, vanilla and strawberry head covering. It seemed that Gunsmith Ghouls was telling the truth. He asked warily, 'Magic in what way? What does it *do*?'

'It is the cowl of invisibility.'

'You mean that if I wear it, I will appear to disappear?' The Growl mulled over these words and said, '"Appear to disappear" is a quaint thing to say, isn't it? But I guess I said it, pard.'

Gunsmith Ghouls grinned a silent reply.

'How does it work, exactly?' demanded The Growl, and he received a tiny shrug in reply and a big pout.

'How should I know? I sell the items that come to me. Sometimes I adjust them. But I don't actually *design* or *make* them. I told you all this already. I am even less responsible for the cowl than I am for the puppets. Objects are donated or sold to me and I sell them on.'

'Who gave you the cowl?' asked The Growl.

'Your guess is as good as mine.'

'You don't know?'

'Of course I know. I just said his name.'

'I didn't hear it.'

'Yoorgez Izaz Gudazmyn.'

The Growl said:

'That's a mighty peculiar name, pard.'

Gunsmith grew annoyed and the meekness he had demonstrated so far was at risk of vanishing. He cried:

'What do you expect? People all over the country have strange names. The United States is rife with weird cognomens. There are men alive today who are called Rip, Duke or Spike. My own real name is bizarre. I was called Bodmas Coincidence when I was a child. My best friend at school was called Monument Backalley. My pa's best friend was called Chickadee Horseflesh. My uncle was called Fastidious Autobiography and *his* uncle was named Rot Gut. I even knew a fella named Moonshine Duck.'

'OK, I get it. Some fella with a weird name sold you the cowl and it just so happens to be a magic cowl. I can live with that. It's a cowl of invisibility, huh? I might just try it on and see what happens. Or *fail to see* what happens, bearing in mind it'll make me invisible.'

He stooped and picked up the cowl and very deftly he flung off the cowl he was already wearing. The new cowl fitted him perfectly. That was good. But his vision suddenly went dark and that was awful. He shouted and stumbled about the room in a sudden panic. He had put the cowl on the wrong way round, with the opening facing backwards.

But that wasn't the real reason he couldn't see anything now. It was more complex and technical than that.

'You tricked me! I have gone blind!'

Gunsmith said, 'Shh! Calm yourself. There's no need to panic. The cowl has indeed made your head invisible. It doesn't make your entire body invisible because it isn't big enough.'

'Just my head? What's the use of that?'

'Well, it's not great.'

'Why can't I see? Why am I blind?'

It seemed to an outside observer that The Growl was a headless corpse that was dancing around the interior of the shop. Gunsmith had to raise his voice to be heard over the stamping feet.

'Your head is invisible. This means that light rays pass right through your skull. They also pass right through your eyes. Now how do eyes work? They're lenses that refract and focus light onto the optic nerve, which sends impressions to the brain. That's what seeing is. But if those light rays aren't focussed onto an optic nerve, no sense impressions can be relayed. That is why you can't see. The blindness is temporary. Remove the cowl and you will be able to see again. It's quite unnecessary to throw a tantrum.'

The Growl ripped off the cowl and threw it far.

'You expect me to buy it?'

'Why not? It's a magic garment, very rare.'

'But it's useless!'

'I never said it was *useful*, did I? Now allow me to tell you a story. Here, in New Orleans, we are no longer in the West and I suppose you are missing it, for it's a fact that the West gets into the blood of those who live there for any length of time. My story concerns two men who lived in California. They happened to be in possession of two drums –'

'Not California again! I can't bear to hear another

word about that state. I am sick of it. Let me shoot you.'

'Wait! My story concerns two men who lived in Nebraska. They both had drums of unusual manufacture. In fact I sold them those drums years earlier. It's safe to say that they were among the best drummers who have ever walked the soil of this grand land of ours.'

And The Growl listened reluctantly.

The names of the two men were Crock and Brawls (Gunsmith said) and those drums had originally come from West Africa. How they ended up in my shop in New Orleans is anyone's guess. Well, maybe not anyone's. People allergic to the act of guessing, who come out in hives whenever they are in the vicinity of a guess, aren't included in that equation.

The drums had cords wrapped around them.

What is the point of cords on the outside of a drum? The question, which I know you wanted to ask, is easily answered. By twisting the cords, the pitch of the drum can be raised or lowered.

Crock and Brawls were lawmen, but that doesn't mean they didn't love all kinds of music. But what they loved more than music was anything that might make the life of a lawman easier.

Crock would often stare at the sun and say, 'No sweat,' while Brawls was a little more down to earth and would say, 'Actually, it's a bit sweaty.' That's how they crisscrossed Nebraska. In fact they were from Idaho originally. But who cares about trivial details? I don't, not really. They wandered the land and sometimes they were separated by circumstances. Maybe they had to chase two different outlaws at the same time.

Crock would follow the trail of one outlaw, Brawls would follow the trail of the other outlaw. Sometimes they would catch them, sometimes not. But they discovered that they could still communicate with each other over the distance by using the drums to 'talk'. I guess this is why those types of drums are known as talking drums? Yes, that's right.

By altering the pitch of the drums by applying pressure to the cords, which in turn tighten or slacken the drumheads, they could produce a vast variety of sounds on any musical scale. In fact, microtones were possible on those drums, notes between the normal notes of Western music, and when I say 'Western' in this context, I mean the east coast of the United States and all of Europe too, I don't just mean the shoot-out zones. Western music, that is classical music. The drums could play *more* notes than a piano could, or a flute or oboe or bassoon, or even a trombone, if used skilfully.

That's right. The drums were like the human voice. Not quite the same but close enough. And the sound carried far, especially when canyons amplified it. Crock could bash out a message such as, 'No sweat,' and Brawls could listen to it, interpret it, and reply with, 'Actually it's a bit sweaty.' Think of the miracle of this exchange! There are no telegraph lines in that part of Nebraska, no way of communicating between remote parts of the state. But these two lawmen had found a method! It was magnificent.

The cords around the drums began to fray and break and fall apart. Crock and Brawls came together one quiet day and decided to replace them with steel wire. They did this and the drums worked just as well. Then two outlaws had to be apprehended and these two outlaws rode off in different directions and once again the two lawmen were split apart. 'No sweat,' opined Crock, and Brawls responded with, 'Actually it's a bit sweaty,' because, as should be obvious now, that was their signature exchange. Crime-fighting duos had signature exchanges back then, maybe they still do, I'm a bit out of touch so I can't say for sure. The lawmen rode off after those outlaws.

Outlaws, inlaws. It's all the same in the Old West. The chase was long and the sun was hot. The steel wires around the drums heated up and slowly started to expand, because that's what metals do if you raise their temperature. Crock would bash out a message to Brawls and Brawls would receive it and bash out a message to Crock, but as the wires expanded and became slacker, so the tone of the drums became lower. Looser drumheads mean a deeper sound. The pitch of the words went down. Treble shouts became bass rumbles. This was fine, there were no problems yet. It was all good.

Or rather, it should have been no trouble, but as time passed and the cables of steel grew slacker, the content of the messages changed. They were no longer straightforward messages about chasing the outlaws. They began to include rude words here and there, blasphemies and cussings, even profanities such as 'bum' and 'plonker'. Now Crock and Brawls weren't too bothered by this at first. We should remember that they were hardened lawmen. They had heard much worse in saloons and cathouses, especially when playing chess against showgirls, but it was disturbing all the same, just a little.

One evening, when both lawmen had been successful in catching the outlaw they were chasing and tying him up, they were camping next to a three-log fire, the only kind of fire worth having out in the West, and under the influences of the big and bright stars they grew misty eyed and nostalgic for the days when it was normal for them to ride as a duo. They decided to hold a conversation with each other across the dividing distance.

'No sweat,' was Crock's opening gambit, and Brawls replied to this with, 'Actually it's a bit sweaty,' and then Crock flexed his fingers and banged out the following observation, 'My bum is aching and my plonker is burning and my mouth tastes like the rear end of a coyote,' to which Brawls answered, 'My knees smell like rancid cactus juice and my midriff is a goddamn son of a torso bitch,' to which Crock said, 'What about your bum, you dung cake? I talked about my bum but you ain't said nothing about yours. What do you think I am? Some kind of bum hobo?' to which Brawls said, 'Keep your hair on, you bum plonker! You putrid bum percussionist!'

As you can imagine, the conversation went downhill from that point on. It was supposed to be a friendly exchange of pleasantries, a bonding between two old friends, companions of the trail, buddies of the law, but it ended up as the noisiest slanging match ever heard in Nebraska. The word 'bum' was sounded a total of ninety-seven times, the word 'plonker' fifty-one times, the word 'twit' thirty-six times, and the insults, 'Above Snakes', 'Slow as molasses in January', 'Bluebelly', 'Bottom-Feeder' and 'Grass-Bellied' a dozen times each. What an argument! It was a night of denigration.

Later, the two men reconciled. They were buddies again and Crock would squint at the sun, or the moon if the sun wasn't available, and say, 'No sweat,' and Brawls would answer, 'Actually it's a bit sweaty,' but in the meantime the drums castigated each other with blows, and in fact at one point during the night of horrid exchanges, Brawls drummed the words, 'Actually it's a bit *sweary*', a clever and apt comment on what was happening, but Crock missed the play on words and responded angrily, 'Bum!'

'Buttocks!' pounded Brawls. 'Rear end!' slammed Crock. 'Derrière,' was Brawls' response, for he had spent time in Louisiana and could *parler Français* like a native, or *comme un natif*, and I don't mean a native of France but one of the original inhabitants of the Louisiana area, the Chitimacha people. He spoke French badly, in other words, or *autrement dit*, as they say in France, but he had never been in France, so let's forget it.

You want to know why they were insulting each other this night of nights? I can tell you why. Crock and Brawls were best friends, they had nothing but a manly regard for each other, but the drums insisted on being rude and uncouth. Why did the drums insist on this? Bear in mind that the steel cables that altered the pitch of the drums had expanded in the heat, loosening the tension of both drumheads. Less tension means slacker membranes which means a lower pitch which means a conversation in the bass range of human hearing. Do you get it now? I can sum it up for you easily.

Yes, that's right. Slack cables had *lowered the tone of the conversation*. I wonder if you had anticipated this all along? The exasperated expression that can be discerned on your face suggests to me that you were expecting such an ending to the story, or an ending of a similar kind, and you aren't satisfied with it, nor with the narrative as a whole?

Well, yes you can shoot me, if you really want to. And no, I don't suppose my story really was a proper story. It was just an excuse for a lame punchline. Fine, I can take criticism. But there *is* a proper story within the story I've told just now.

Wait a moment and don't squeeze that trigger just yet! The true story is still waiting to be related. We haven't reached that part yet. I'm not bluffing or stalling, honest. Listen to me, please! Don't pull that trigger. If you do, I'll never be able to let you know what happens. And it's a great story, an unusual tale, something really quite special.

Thank you! I appreciate your patience. Before the night of the argument between the drums, just a few weeks before, Crock and Brawls happened to be chasing two other outlaws in a different part of Nebraska. They were separated again and they made camp and felt lonely. They had a drum conversation but the drumheads were tight this time and there was no rudeness in anything they said to each other. Crock decided to tell Brawls a story. It was a story he heard years before he'd met Brawls, a story about the sunset. Brawls wanted to hear it and so Crock pounded on his drum.

The story he told went as follows. Once there was a cowboy who lived on the coast at Big Sur. He loved the sunset because all cowboys love it. He hated it when the sunset was over and the night happened. If he could have wished for anything at all, he would have wished for the sunset to remain fixed in place in the sky, for the sunset to be permanent. He didn't like the way the sun slipped down behind the horizon. This phenomenon irked him. He wondered if there was anything he could do about it?

After a lot of thought, he decided that yes, there

was something he could do. He knew a fisherman who lived in a shack and he went to him and asked to borrow his rod and line. He waited for the sun to start setting in the sea off Big Sur and he cast his line at the sun. The hook stuck in the sun itself and then the cowboy started reeling it in. Not easy work! The sun was harder than any fish any man has ever landed. It was tougher than a barracuda or a hemingway, even tougher than a shark or an ichthyosaur, and while there's nothing worse than an itch you can't scratch, an ichthyosaur you can't catch is almost as bad. But this cowboy was a determined young fella.

The rod bent and almost snapped, but the hook was secure and the muscles in the cowboy's arms were good enough for the task. The sun stopped setting. It was fixed in the sky. The man jammed the rod into the ground and supported it with rocks. Now the sun was tethered like a mad bull. The cowboy thanked the fisherman who lived in the shack. He offered him money but the fishermen had no use for dollars out here in Big Sur.

The only way the cowboy could repay the fisherman was by telling him a story. So he started a long narrative about a train robber who – Hang on, don't get angry with me! Why don't you want to hear the cowboy's story? It's rather amusing, I can promise you that. Really, you ought to be more patient and let me narrate this new adventure. Why are you so eager to shoot me? Come on, I really think you'll love this new story …

'Sorry,' said The Growl, 'but enough is enough.'

Gunsmith Ghouls sighed.

'I thought you might say something like that, but I had to try. Anyway, be aware that the cowl of invisibility *is* useful. You can throw it over the heads of enemies or get them to wear it back to front, as you did. Then they'll be unable to see. It's a weapon, I guess.'

'Why did you tell me that story, pard?'

'I wanted to distract you and buy time, just as Scheherazade did in those old stories. You know the legend?'

'Huh? Lemonade?'

'I'm talking about Scheherazade, not lemonade. She married a cruel king named Shahryar who planned to kill her the morning after their wedding night but she told him amusing stories.'

The Growl nodded.

'Of course I know. She drew out the tales and he was so keen to hear the endings that he kept sparing her life. But what connection does that have with our situation? I am definitely going to kill you. If you draw out your tales too much I will just shoot you anyway.'

'Well, I wanted to delay the terrible moment.'

'Until what? A rescue?'

'Sort of. I thought that if enough time passed one of The Sideliners might extend his arm and push you out of the action, sidelining you and saving me. It was a slim hope but a hope nonetheless. They do things like that, you know, and people have been saved by them.'

'The hope is so slim it has died of malnutrition,' said The Growl, 'because I happen to know that The Sideliners no longer exist. They sidelined themselves by accident very recently. Sorry.'

'I never liked that gang anyway. They tried to sideline me once. Luckily it was just one of my puppets that they sidelined. But that was after I had been so nice to them. It was me who sold them the device that makes the horses beneath the platform they ride on invisible. Can you believe it? I provided the projector but they still tried to sideline me.'

'It's a tough old world. Your time is up, Gunsmith Ghouls. Telling me the stories was a waste of breath.'

'Fair enough. But don't you ever waste *your* breath?'

'On occasion, pard.'

'Will you give me an example?'

'Why not? I could tell you a story of my own. Most of the men beasts who have studied with shamans are good persons, but infrequently one of 'em might be tempted by the dark side. I knew a fella like that who was a mouse-man. His name was The Squeak. I crept up on him one night when he was pointing a gun at an innocent traveller and I drew my own gun and I coughed, dainty-like. He turned his head and was shocked to see me. I said, "Squeak now or forever hold your piece", and what I meant was that he had to squeak an apology to the man he was assaulting or I would glue his gun to his hand and he'd never be able to get it off. The Squeak squeaked.'

'I don't blame him. Will you tell me another story?'

'I certainly won't.'

'Will you make duck noises for half an hour?'

'I decline that pleasure.'

'Ah well, it was worth a try, wasn't it?'

'Not really, no.'

Gunsmith Ghouls shrugged resignedly.

The Growl shot him.

But once again, he was only a puppet.

'Another automaton? Dang! That means my quest still isn't over. But that means my own life has been spared too. So maybe I shouldn't complain. But I intend to complain anyway!'

Yet he remained silent after this outburst.

And he stood still.

He didn't move for many minutes. He was exactly like a statue, a statue of a sculptor. He was utterly immobile. Even his panting wasn't discernible. It was as if something inside him had broken. His mind whirled but his body refused to budge so much as one inch.

'There is a town on the coast of Alabama that is called *Mobile* but you are *Immobile*,' observed a voice.

This interruption broke the spell.

The Growl blinked. Gunsmith Ghouls walked through the door at the rear of the shop. He smiled at the dog-man but received only a sigh in reply. Clearly The Growl was demoralised.

'You are just a puppet too, huh?'

'No, I am the real Gunsmith Ghouls. Almost. Yes, I admit it. I am a puppet but the last one. After me there is only the real person. And I'm not like any of the other puppets you've killed.'

'What's so different about you, pard?'

'I am not mechanical. There's no clockwork or chemicals inside me. I am a more primitive type of mannequin. I am worked from inside by a man, by the real Gunsmith Ghouls, in fact. You might say that I am a costume rather than a proper puppet. A clever disguise.'

'I have only one more bullet. I was planning to use it on myself but then I changed my mind. I could use it on you, but what if I need it for later? I think I will destroy you with my teeth.'

'Always thought your bark was worse than your bite, but maybe not. Sure, I can fight you. But first let me say that the other puppet didn't get the story that he told you right. He made some errors. The cowboy who fished for the sunset? His name was Flinger Doops. He cast his link and the hook sank into the sun but the sun's setting was too powerful to be stopped and because he kept a tight grip on the rod, he was dragged after it. Round and round the world he went, pulled always by the eternally setting sun.'

'And so?' The Growl was dismissive.

'He's still in orbit. I kid you not. Maybe one day,

just before sunset, if you look up, you might see him endlessly circling our planet. Flinger Doops, that's him. Round and round. The fisher of the sunset. It just goes to show how weird this age of ours is. That's the end.'

The Growl nodded. He unsheathed his teeth by curling his lips. He issued no warning before flinging himself at Gunsmith Ghouls. The puppet went down immediately, unable to resist the weight and power of the man-dog. The Growl went for the puppet's chest instead of his throat, as most hounds would do. His fangs bit deep and tore a hole in his enemy's sternum. Then with his hands he widened the hole and exposed the hiding place of the man inside. But the inside was bare. There was just hollowness.

'But you are empty inside! You said you were just a costume for the real Gunsmith Ghouls, the real man!'

'I never said he was a man. He's real but he's not a man. Oh no! He is far greater than any man could be. And Gunsmith Ghouls isn't even his real name. It's the pseudonym of a pseudonym.'

'Tell me his name!'

'You have already met him …'

'Who is he?'

'He is called Monkey Man!'

'What! But he was just a disciple of a shaman, the same as myself. He's no greater than I am, or than Doug was, or any beast-man who learned with any of the Mojave wizards. He is just –'

'That's incorrect. He never studied with a shaman.'

'You mean to say –'

'Yes. He was *always* a Monkey Man!'

'But that means –'

The Growl had no idea what it meant, nor did Gunsmith Ghouls, who was rapidly dying, his mouth closing forever, so they left the statement hanging and directed their attention to other matters. The puppet raised its head very slowly and grinned sourly. It spoke:

'You are a puppet too, you know.'

'What? But –'

'I'm not lying. You are an automaton, not an organic being. Just like your boss, Ridley Smart, you are a puppet who went wrong. Your consciousness is so strong that it overrides the consciousness of the person you really are. Does that make sense? There is a man alive today who was used as a model for a puppet. You are the model but the moment you were activated, your sense of self, which was mighty, overrode his sense of self. So you became Bill Bones and then The Growl and forgot who you really were. The moment you die, you will revert to being your original self. Honest.'

The Growl was shocked. It was a ludicrous statement and yet deep down it resonated with him. He felt it was true. He wondered who he 'really' was. Did this mean he ought to use the last bullet on himself and find out? He wanted to question the puppet that was just a costume, but the mouth of that weird entity, if entity it was, was now saying:

'Monkey Man is the rightful occupant of this suit that resembles a puppet that looks like Gunsmith Ghouls, but one day he decided to leave it to its own devices and go off to play chess with showgirls on a paddle steamer set high in the treetops in a redwood forest. You know all about this. I am just the *absence* of Monkey Man, but Monkey Man is so marvellous that even his absence has thought, strength and cunning.'

He revealed one more thing before he died.

Coughing weakly, he said:

'You are leaving the shop now. Up until a few days ago there was a very elaborate trap for people such as you. A tripwire would activate a spring that would cause a musket to fire. The vibration of the musket would topple pegs into a bowl that would tip over and knock a ball down a ramp, and so on, and finally a crossbow would discharge a bolt at you. It was all very fine, but the component pieces were sold to a customer. My fang shrank and all went well. No trap remains for you, Bill.'

'Don't call me that. I am The Growl.'

The puppet was dead.

The Growl walked to the door, pulled it open savagely and stepped through it briskly and without looking back.

He was in the street now. It was early evening.

The sun was setting.

A movement high overhead caught his attention. A man was flying on the end of a line. He was dressed in cowboy clothes. Flinger Doops? With a snarl that was utterly devoid of mercy, The Growl aimed his gun at the speck. Then he squeezed the trigger. The man slumped and let go of the line. He plummeted to the ground, somewhere far beyond the limits of New Orleans. This was the last bullet. The Growl grumbled:

'I didn't save it for myself after all.'

He walked away.

He turned a corner and a figure was approaching him. It grinned and aimed a revolver at him. It was an outlaw.

'Howdy, my name is Kirk Doings and I been paid to kill you, Mister Dog. Some guy called Monkey Man hired me. He said I'd probably find you here in this street but I got a bit lost.'

'Easy to get lost in New Orleans.'

'Huh? Easy to saddle a hoss with beans?'

'That's not what I said.'

'Eh? What's not a water bed?'

'Get it over with, pard. This is annoying.'

'Sure is. Goodnight.'

The gun exploded and The Growl felt a great weight descend on him. Then he remembered the cowl of invisibility. He threw it and it landed on the head of his assailant, who began shouting:

'Hey, I can't see a goddamn thing here!'

But it was too late.

The Growl was dying. He felt his mind closing. And yet at the same time a light filled his inner vision. He saw stars in a sky that wasn't the sky above him right now. His consciousness was shifting from his present form, which was just a puppet, back to his real self.

What would that real self be like?

He would find out soon enough. He was slipping away. He fell down, eyes dimming, breath stopped in his chest. A beautiful weakness overcame him. His limbs grew heavy and he felt himself melting into nothingness. Yet a new reality was opening for him at the same time. No, not a new reality but an old one, the life he had once had. His truth.

The Lord lay back on the deck of his yacht and gazed at the night sky. Soon the artillery shell from the massive cannon on the west coast of California, near the town of Punta Arena, would be passing overhead, on its way to smash the White House into crumbs. He felt more conscious of everything around him than he'd felt in a long time. Almost as if he had been sleepwalking the past few years. It was a wild sensation, invigorating!

He had reached his destination in *The Bounder* some hours earlier and the vessel was riding at anchor. The islet of Es Vedrà loomed near. He was waiting for the projectile to pass directly overhead, fizzing and whizzing like a cricket ball made of phosphorus. How he adored receiving joy on his back! Surely the most satisfying position for it? He hummed to himself as he waited. A patriotic tune he had composed himself.

Then one of his retainers shouted and he turned his head. The meteor was rising in the east, climbing over the horizon and it was even more beautiful than he had expected it to be. Bright white, yes, but speckled with pale green. 'Say farewell to the White House!' He held up a brimming glass of Champagne. But the bubbles were few and far between in the liquid now. He toasted the sky and the fiery doom soaring through it.

The projectile didn't stop climbing. It didn't level off. It followed the exact trajectory necessary to cross thousands more miles of ocean and smash directly into the White House. It passed overhead in a blaze of emerald glory. The Lord laughed. His three retainers, despite their dignified demeanours, also cheered. It was difficult not to feel jubilant.

In the shadow of the islet of Es Vedrà the little celebration continued for a few more hours. Then The Lord ordered *The Bounder* to set sail back to the port of Tarragona. When he reached it he heard the news. The White House had been smashed to bits. The British government had decided to take this opportunity to launch a full scale invasion of the United States of America. Already a fleet was being assembled. The Lord was being offered the rank of Fleet Admiral and the Queen begged him to accept the role.

The Lord laughed. Of course he would accept. And then for some baffling reason, he threw back his head and growled at the moon. Why did he do this? A temporary fit of madness? Yes, that was the only sensible answer. Without more ado, he made preparations for his return to Britain. His exile was finally over. It was his dream come true. The reclaiming of the USA for the British Empire! A day unequalled in all modern history.

He ruffled his hair with his hand and just for a moment he wondered why he was bare headed. Shouldn't he be wearing a cowl? Then he frowned. Why a cowl? That was one of the most ridiculous garments ever devised. No, he was The Lord and wore only top hats, a top hat of inordinate height, in fact, so high that he always had to stoop when walking under bridges. The tallest hat in the history of the world. When he became Fleet Admiral his hat would be different, of course. It would resemble an inverted canoe. There wasn't much he could do about that. No worries. It was Destiny.

The moon shone on his upturned face. He was happy.

And so was his monarch.

Queen Victoria paraded through the shattered streets of Washington DC in an ornately gilded chariot pulled by a tame lion. It should have been pulled by a lion and a unicorn too, but unicorns simply weren't available in this day and age. Maybe they never had been.

The Lord rode in the chariot by her side.

They had landed on the shores of the United States six months earlier. A series of sea battles had been fought, followed by many land campaigns. The British armed forces had been reduced by half, but the American forces were in complete disarray. Resistance fighters were still active in the various mountain ranges, but the cities were British.

The Lord had proved to be a most excellent Fleet Admiral. His flagship, which for mysterious reasons he had named *The Growl*, had sailed among the enemy vessels, blasting them left and right until they were matchwood. It was incredible. The figurehead on the prow of his ship was carved in the likeness of a dog, once again no one knew why.

Not even The Lord understood his own inclinations. But he didn't worry about them. The days of worrying were over. The days of drinking American bourbon and playing chess against showgirls were just beginning. His admiral hat had been shot full of holes but he still wore it proudly for the parade. When the procession was over, he would return to his top hat and because the skies here were so much bigger, he wondered if he could even double its height, a hat that scraped the underside of clouds.

The lion pulling the chariot yawned and stopped in its tracks. It curled up and went to sleep. Queen Victoria jerked the reins and it woke up and resumed the journey towards the crater where the White House had once stood. With a sigh, she muttered, 'Useless beast!'

'A unicorn would help immensely, ma'am.'

'But they are mythical.'

'I have been making inquiries, your majesty. I have learned that one does exist. It wasn't always a unicorn. It was once a woman called Jalamity Kane. I have sent out men to capture her.'

'And she is adequately unicorny, is she?'

'So rumours suggest.'

'Very well. I look forward to seeing her.'

The Lord bowed.

She regarded him for a moment and said:

'The United States is once again part of the British Empire. But I suppose that the countries of South America will be wondering what might alter in terms of trade. They will be seeking reassurance. I believe that you would make a very efficient envoy of the crown. What do you say? Are you willing to travel there? I hear that it can be rather pleasant.'

'Certainly, ma'am. It would be an honour.'

'You will be based in Buenos Aires. That is in Argentina, I think. Do you suppose you will be ready to leave next week? There is a steamer leaving early on Monday morning from Chesapeake Bay. We will have to get a new uniform for you and a new hat, of course.'

'I was rather hoping to be able to wear a hat of my own design. A top hat approximately one mile high.'

Queen Victoria considered this and nodded. 'It seems like a good idea but wouldn't the weight of it crush your skull into your shoulders, distorting bones in your thoracic spine and rendering you unfit for service and possibly deader than a doornail? Could this be?'

'My life has already been full of risks, ma'am. This is a risk I'm willing to take for the sake of the Empire.'

The Queen was grave. 'We are *very* amused.'

'Thank you, ma'am.'

'Can you do an impression of a duck?'

'Yes, your majesty.'

'Why not do one right now?'

The Lord bowed. Then he squeezed his lips together and tried to quack. It should have worked perfectly but something went wrong. For some reason the sound resembled a growl. But Queen Victoria found this most amusing. Taking off her crown and swinging it around on the end of a windmilling arm, she was unable to control her wilder impulses. She began growling too. The Lord soon stopped, his jaws aching, but she continued, then the growls turned into barking. The lion looked back over its shoulder.

British flags waved from every window in the street. And now there in the distance was the blackened crater.

It was still smoking.

'That gigantic gun of yours was a very good idea,' she said as she studied the rubble and the destruction.

'Thanks, but to be honest it wasn't my idea.'

'Really? Then who?'

'Some chap by the name of Ridley Smart. He was

a newspaper editor and one day he wrote an editorial outlining the danger to the United States of an enormous gun situated on the Californian coast that could lob a projectile all the way around most of the circumference of the planet and turn the White House into motes of dust. He wanted to warn people. Nobody listened. Apart from me, that is. But instead of heeding his warning, I took the idea and employed it for my own purposes. Yours too.'

'That's very interesting,' said Queen Victoria.

'Yes,' agreed The Lord.

'Are you sure you can do duck impressions?'

'I don't know, ma'am.'

But she didn't press the point, and a few days later The Lord found himself bound for Argentina on a packet steamer, standing on the deck and watching as the coastline of the United States vanished behind him. He was in such an elated mood that he began singing as they ploughed through the waves, a sea shanty he had picked up in his dissolute youth. The noise attracted sailors, who came first to listen and then to dance sombrely in circles while making duck noises. After an hour, The Lord stopped singing.

The sailors scattered in different directions, returning to their duties. The Lord was left alone. The day was over. Night was drawing on rapidly. The moon rose and it resembled the face of a dog. How strange! The misty halo around it looked like a cowl. The effect was eerie.

A strange idea appeared in the mind of The Lord.

His belly button itched. What if this reality wasn't real? What if the external cosmos was only his inner reality? He shuddered as the moon shimmered.

The Lord thumbed his nose at it and, his composure regained, went below to find his supper, a bottle of rum, a chessboard and, assuming there were no showgirls on board, a cabin boy. He chuckled.

His story is history. History is his story.

And that's the end.

About the Author

Rhys Hughes was born in Wales but has lived in many different countries and currently lives in India. He began writing fiction at an early age and his first book, *Worming the Harpy*, was published in 1995. Since that time he has published more than forty other books. He recently completed an ambitious project that involved writing exactly 1000 linked narratives and took more than thirty years. His work has been translated into ten languages.

Also Available From Telos Publishing

RHYS HUGHES
Captains Stupendous
Steampunk adventure novel

The Wistful Wanderings of Perceval Pitthelm

RAVEN DANE

THE MISADVENTURES OF CYRUS DARIAN
Steampunk Adventure Series
1: Cyrus Darian And The Technomicron
2: Cyrus Darian And The Ghastly Horde
3: Cyrus Darian And The Wicked Wraith

Death's Dark Wings
Stand alone alternative history novel

Absinthe & Arsenic
Horror and fantasy short story collection

SOLOMON STRANGE
The Haunting of Gospall

SAM STONE
KAT LIGHTFOOT MYSTERIES
Steampunk adventure series
1: Zombies at Tiffany's
2: Kat on a Hot Tin Airship
3: What's Dead PussyKat
4: Kat of Green Tentacles
5: Kat and the Pendulum
6: Ten Little Demons

The Complete Lightfoot (limited hardback edition of all six novellas, plus bonus material)

If you have enjoyed this book and would like more information about other Telos titles, then check the website below.

TELOS PUBLISHING
www.telos.co.uk

Printed in Great Britain
by Amazon